Stand-up

Other Walker and Company Titles by
Robert J. Randisi

Separate Cases
Hard Look

Stand-up

A Miles Jacoby Mystery

Robert J. Randisi

Walker and Company
New York

First published in the United States of America in 1994
by Walker Publishing Company, Inc.

Published simultaneously in Canada by Thomas Allen & Son
Canada, Limited, Markham, Ontario

Library of Congress Cataloging-in-Publication Data
Randisi, Robert J.
Stand-up / Robert J. Randisi.
p.   cm. — (A Miles Jacoby mystery)
ISBN 0-8027-3196-1
1. Jacoby, Miles (Fictitious character)—Fiction.
2. Private investigators—New York (N.Y.)—Fiction. I. Title.
II. Series: Randisi, Robert J. Miles Jacoby mystery.
PS3568.A53S73   1994
813'.54—dc20   94-18377
CIP

Printed in the United States of America
2 4 6 8 10 9 7 5 3 1

To Marthayn
For showing me how
to stand up again

Stand-up

▽

Prologue

Why is it that death is such a part of our everyday life, but when we are confronted with it we're surprised?

From the health club where Joy White worked I walked to her apartment on Horatio Street. I'd interviewed her once already during my search for Ray Carbone, but now I needed to talk to her again. I rang her buzzer but there was no answer. I didn't know where her fire escape was, even if her building had one, so I pressed one of the other buzzers.

"Whataya want?"

"Pizza."

"Didn't order any."

I pressed another.

"Who is it?"

"Pizza."

"What?"

On the fifth buzzer, it worked.

"Pizza."

"It's about time."

They buzzed me in. Somebody's always ordering pizza.

I took the stairs two at a time, feeling a sense of urgency. As I approached Joy's door I didn't know how I was going to get it open, considering the number of locks she had. As it turned out it wasn't a problem. I turned the knob and the door opened.

"Shit."

I didn't have a gun and I didn't know what to expect

inside. I heard a door open on the floor above me and somebody yelled, "Hey, where's my pizza?"

I stepped into Joy's apartment.

The kitchen was a shambles. Somehow the kitchen table had collapsed, the legs flat underneath it, as if a great weight had fallen on it.

There were only three rooms and I could see them all from where I stood. They were the same, torn up as if by a tornado. Or a fight.

I walked through the bedroom into the living room. The mattress had been pulled off the bed, and the sofa cushions were on the floor. None of these items had been slit, so it wasn't as if someone was searching for something. With the table lamps in pieces on the floor, it still looked as if there had been a fight. If there had been, where was the loser?

There was still the bathroom to check. As I opened the door, I saw an arm and a leg hanging out of the tub. I moved closer and saw Joy White lying inside. Her eyes were closed, and the skin around them had been battered and bruised. Blood had dripped from her mouth onto her chin. The clothes she was wearing—a blouse and a pair of jeans—had been torn in a way that was not stylish. The skin on her hands was cracked and bloody, and I could see that some of her nails had been torn.

No question but that she was dead.

I backed out of the bathroom feeling sick, staggered to the phone, and called 911. I then put in a call to a friend of mine, Detective Hocus from the Major Case Squad, and told him that I might need a reference.

"What else is new?"

$\triangledown$

1

WALKER BLUE AND I had worked together—sort of—a few years ago, but since that time we'd seen very little of each other.

Walker is generally considered to be the best private investigator in New York. He may even be the best in the business. That's why I found it curious to receive an invitation from him to have lunch at the Russian Tea Room about a week or so before finding Joy White's body in her bathtub.

Okay, I admit it. I'd never been inside the Russian Tea Room, on Fifty-seventh Street, just to the left of Carnegie Hall. I'd passed it many times and had almost given in to the urge to peek inside, but even doing that would have made me feel foolish. I've just never had the kind of clientele, or business, that warranted eating there. The fanciest place I'd eaten with a client had probably been the Top of the Sixes, the very top of 666 Fifth Avenue—certainly not on a par with the Russian Tea Room or with Tavern on the Green, The Rainbow Room, or The Four Seasons, also restaurants I'd never been to.

Slightly intimidated by having lunch in a place that caters to celebrities on a daily basis, I went so far as to wear a tie. Just inside the revolving door is a coat room and a maitre d's stand. Off the right is the stairway that leads up to the cabaret.

"Can I help you, sir?" the maitre d' asked. He had the good taste not to look down his nose at me, even though he might have—I was grossly out of place.

"Yes, I'm meeting someone."

"May I ask whom?"

"Walker Blue?"

"Ah, yes, Mr. Blue has arrived. This way, please."

He led me past the red leather booths which I had only previously seen when somebody—who was it?—made me watch Dustin Hoffman in *Tootsie*. Walker was sitting at a table for four, looking at ease and comfortable—and much thinner than I remembered him. There was also more gray in his hair, which still came to a wicked widow's peak.

"Mr. Blue? Your guest has arrived."

Walker looked up. "Thanks, Henry."

Henry turned to me. "Enjoy your lunch, sir."

"Thank you."

He held my chair. There was already a menu waiting for me on the table.

One of the things I liked about Walker was that, as in control as he was of every situation, he did not take liberties.

For instance, he said to me, "I haven't ordered yet. I thought you'd like to look at the menu."

"Thanks, Walker."

Since he had obviously decided what he was going to have, I made a quick choice and picked chicken Kiev. The waiter came over, wearing red trousers and a white cossack shirt. We gave our order—Walker ordered goulash—and for a drink I ordered a Russian beer. The waiter told me the brand, but I forgot it the moment he walked away. Walker had been nursing a glass of white wine while waiting for me, and now he ordered a vodka that was a specialty of the house.

I took a long look at him. He was wearing a double-breasted charcoal-gray suit that looked like silk. Knowing Walker, it probably was, as was the tie. Walker had always been a sharp dresser, but I thought he needed some color.

"If you don't mind me saying so, Walker, you look thinner than I remember."

"And grayer," he added, touching his hair lightly. "The

truth of the matter is I'm grayer because I'm older. I'm thinner, however, because I recently had a heart attack."

"I'm sorry, I didn't know."

He waved my apology away impatiently.

"My doctor advised losing weight, if you can believe it."

"And you're having goulash?"

He eyed me peevishly for a moment.

"Hey, it's none of my business."

"Every so often," he said, carefully, "I treat myself—like today."

"Fine. Maybe you can treat me now?"

He looked a question at me.

"Tell me why you called me? We don't usually run in the same circles."

"We are not so different, you and I."

That surprised me.

"In fact, it is my heart attack, in part, that prompted me to call you."

"How so?"

"I've been thinking of expanding."

"Expanding."

"My practice."

Lawyers have practices, so do doctors. I never thought of a private investigator as having a practice.

"In what way?"

"I would like to take someone on to share the workload."

"Someone?"

"Well . . . obviously, I am offering the position to you first."

"Me?"

A second surprise.

The waiter came with our drinks. He set my beer and a glass down in front of me. Walker's vodka was served in what looked like a small vase, and that was set in a bowl of crushed ice. Next to it the waiter set a small glass.

"Thank you, Henry."

As Henry left I said, "You eat here a lot?"

"Occasionally I meet clients here," Walker said. "You would not have to do that if you didn't want to."

"What would I have to do, Walker?"

"Basically what you do now, only for more money."

It was not said as an insult, just a fact.

"You would bring in cases and work on them. On occasion I would bring in a case that we would both have to work on. Um, there will be the odd occasion when something, uh, physical would have to be done. That would fall to you."

"Are we talking about strong-arm stuff?" I asked. I felt the hair on my neck bristle.

"No, no . . ." He sat back and seemed annoyed, more with himself than with me. "I'm talking about things I can no longer do because of my . . . condition. Surveillance, long trips out of town, that sort of thing."

"I see."

It bothered Walker to have to do this. He'd been running an extremely successful one-man shop for years, once in a while subcontracting a job out when he needed help. Having to hire someone full-time to do the thing he used to do irked him, and I could see why.

"I have a question."

"Because you are reliable, intelligent, and honest."

I stared at him.

"You were about to ask why you, isn't that correct?"

"Yes, it is."

"Well, that's my answer."

"And now you want mine."

"Not right away. We can eat lunch, and then when you leave you can think it over."

"I would like to think it over. I mean, it's a big move for me. I'm used to working for myself. I don't think I'd be real good at punching a time clock—"

"You don't understand."

"I don't?"

"No. I am not asking you to become my employee. I am asking you to become my partner."

I was speechless, and tried to cover that fact by taking in some beer.

"A full partner?"

"Well, not quite a full partner, but we can work out percentages later. I would like to maintain the controlling interest . . . but your name would go on the door."

"Blue & Jacoby?"

He winced, and I couldn't blame him. It sounded awful.

"I don't think that would be necessary, Walker. If I came aboard I think you should keep the name 'Walker Blue Investigations'."

"Or we could go to 'Walker Blue Associates'."

"That would be fine, too . . . if I come aboard."

"Naturally."

"I mean, now that I know you're talking about a partnership it's an even bigger decision."

"I understand that."

The waiter came with lunch and we waited while he placed steaming plates on the table.

I had been working on my own since the death of my friend and mentor, Eddie Waters. It was during my investigation of Eddie's death that I had originally met Walker, who respected Eddie tremendously. Since then I had quit boxing to work as a full-time investigator, and over the past few years I had been learning my craft. Well, I still had a lot to learn, and who better to learn it from than Walker Blue?

After the waiter had gone I looked at Walker and said, "Okay, I've thought about it."

"You accept my offer?"

"Yes."

"Good," he said with a nod. He poured some of the chilled vodka into his glass and lifted it. "We'll work out the details later. For now, here's to a successful partnership."

I lifted my beer and said, "To success."

Wouldn't that be a nice change?

▽

2

STARTING A PARTNERSHIP does not get accomplished over-
night. Lawyers have to get involved, papers have to be drawn
up and signed—and co-signed—and Walker decided we
would move to a larger location so that we would each have
our own office. He also intended to hire a second woman to
work in the office, basically as my secretary.

So for a few weeks I would still be working out of Packy's,
the bar in the Village I had inherited a little while ago after
Packy, its owner and my friend, was killed.

Working with Walker would undoubtedly put me in
another tax bracket, so I'd probably have to decide if I should
keep the bar.

I enjoy working at Packy's, and I like the people who work
for me—especially my manager, a black female bodybuilder
named Geneva. She is possibly the coolest person I've ever
known. At twenty-four she'd been in New York for almost
four years, working for me for the last six months or so. She'd
moved from New Jersey, so culture shock had not been a
factor. I'd made her my manager after about a month, and
it was working out perfectly.

Both of my bartenders have hit on Geneva mercilessly, but
she knows how to handle them. I hadn't hit on her myself,
yet, but it was hard not to watch her when we were working
the same shift. Knowing her had taught me that female
bodybuilders are not at all unfeminine. Dressed casually, she
looked like any well-toned, beautiful young woman. The
only time she looked muscular was when she pumped herself

up for a contest. In fact, I had attended two of the contests, cheering her on to two top-three finishes. She wants to turn pro eventually, but so far she's just competed in the amateur ranks.

Geneva was one of the few people I told about the partnership with Walker Blue. In fact, I mentioned it to her the next day.

"Who is Walker Blue?"

We were behind the bar, and it was a slow April afternoon. The weather was so nice that we had the door propped open.

"He's probably the best PI in the business."

"Colorful name. Is he like that?"

"You mean colorful? I wouldn't say that. He's very distinguished."

"Distinguished? You mean tight-assed."

Geneva has her own dress code. That day she was wearing a sleeveless purple sweatshirt with a pink spandex sports top underneath. I enjoyed watching the muscles in her forearms and biceps when she was washing glasses. She had taken to wearing baggy tops around the bar because customers would make comments about the fact that she was well endowed. She sometimes complained that the only thing that would keep her from being a champion bodybuilder was "big tits."

"I don't think he's tight-assed . . . exactly."

"So what's this partnership gonna mean for us?"

By "us" she meant herself and our two bartenders, Ed and Marty. Ed had worked the place for Packy, while I had allowed Geneva to hire Marty.

"I don't know yet."

"You mean you'd close Packy's? After all our work?"

I looked around. The place had changed. Packy 'd run it as a shot and a beer bar, but since Geneva had come on board and put some of her ideas into action, we catered to a more upscale crowd, and we'd expanded our menu so we even had a lunch rush . . . sometimes. The place had turned a profit the past two months for the first time since I'd taken it over.

"Not close it."

"Then sell it?"

I hesitated, then said, "I haven't decided what I'm going to do, Gen."

"But you are goin' into partnership with this high-priced, tight-assed dude?"

"I'm going into partnership with Walker, yes."

"Well, you *will* tell us before you do somethin', won't you?" We wouldn't need ice for a week.

"Give me a break, Gen. I won't do anything without telling you guys first."

"You better not."

"I won't."

"Good."

"Good."

"Oh, by the way," she said then, "you got a letter today. It's by the register."

I figured we'd discussed the other matter enough for one day, so I walked over to the cash register. The letter was from Cathy Merrill, a lady cop I'd met in Tampa. She had helped me with a case, and we'd ended up in bed; since then we'd had sort of a long-distance relationship via letters and an occasional phone call. All in all, it was the longest and most successful relationship I'd had in some time, the distance probably being a big factor.

"From that gal of yours in Florida?" Gen asked.

"That's right."

"She comin' here?"

"I haven't read it yet."

Ever since I'd gotten back from Florida and told Geneva about Cathy, she'd been bugging me about when Cathy was going to move north. Sometimes I thought—or maybe hoped—Geneva was jealous. The truth was that Cathy had no intention of moving away from Florida, and I had no intention of moving down there.

"Ain't you gonna read it?"

"Later."

"Hmmph."

"You're so nosy I'm surprised *you* didn't open it." I put the letter in my shirt pocket.

"I tried steamin' it," she said without looking at me, "but that don't always work."

I didn't know whether to believe her or not.

▽

3

STEVE STILWELL AND Bruce Taylor were cops, partners for many years, friends even longer than that. Stilwell was about my height but weighed a good deal less. He had a carefully trimmed beard and mustache and gentle eyes behind wire-rimmed glasses. As was his norm, he was wearing a plain T-shirt and sports jacket with the sleeves shoved up over his elbows. Bruce Taylor, on the other hand, was close to six and a half feet tall and although he had recently lost a lot of the weight that had nestled around his middle, he was far from svelte. He was wearing a pocket T-shirt that had undoubtedly come from a big and tall men's shop, and lightweight slacks.

"You guys are early," I said, leaning on the bar. "What's up?"

They both looked unhappy, but that wasn't unusual. One or the other of them was always complaining about something—only this time it seemed to be something serious.

"We got suspended," Stilwell said.

"Unjustly," Taylor added.

"What for?"

They both sat at the bar and Stilwell said, "IAD is investigating the disappearance of some drugs and cash from a bust of ours that went down weeks ago."

"They finally got around to pullin' our tins this morning," Taylor said, "pending the outcome of the investigation."

"That sucks." I didn't believe either of them would risk

their jobs for some cash and drugs. Being detectives was a drug to these guys, and they wouldn't put that on the line for any other kind of high.

"What are you going to do about it?"

"Well," Stilwell said, "right now we're gonna have a couple of beers and some sandwiches and enjoy our time off."

"You're going to take this lying down?"

Taylor pinned me with his dark eyes. "He didn't say that."

Geneva came out of the kitchen and said, "Hi, boys."

"Hi, Geneva," Stilwell said.

"Got a new beer in. Wanna try it?" she asked.

"What is it?"

"Icehouse."

"One of those ice beers?" Taylor said.

"That's right."

"Bring us two, and a couple of your Geneva specials."

"Comin' up."

Geneva had instituted a special hero sandwich, and while no one except her really knew what was in it, that didn't stop people from ordering it. If I wasn't careful, she was going to make me a rich man.

I left the suspended partners to their beer and sandwiches and went through the kitchen into the office behind it. On my desk were the ledgers, the part of the business I hate. Going into partnership with Walker Blue would certainly rid me of having to deal with that little chore.

Still, Geneva had a point. I couldn't just walk out on her and Marty and Ed. Even if I didn't want to run Packy's anymore, I'd have to find somebody who did.

I wondered if Walker would object to his partner owning a bar.

"Boss?"

Geneva stuck her head in the door.

"Yeah, Gen?"

"Guy out here to see you."

"About what? A bill? I told that liquor guy I'd pay him by—"

"Ain't no liquor guy," Gen said, interrupting. "I think this guy wants to hire you in your, uh, other work."

I frowned. I wasn't sure I wanted to take on any cases until all the papers were signed with Walker. I was sure, though, that I didn't want to go over the ledgers right now.

"I'll be right out. Stick him in the back booth."

I had started using the back booth as an office, a practice I'd no longer have to maintain once Walker and I moved into our new suite.

I went back through the kitchen and came out behind the bar. My visitor sat in the booth with his back against the wall, facing the bar, so I could see his face. He looked vaguely familiar, but at the moment I couldn't place him.

"That guy look familiar to you?" I asked Geneva.

"Not to me," she said. "Looks like just another white guy to me."

Stilwell and Taylor had both turned to take a look, and Stilwell said, "I know who that is."

"You do?"

"Sure. Stan Waldrop."

"Who?" Taylor and I said at the same time.

"Come on, Stan Waldrop. Don't either of you guys have cable TV? You got to get cable in here, Jack."

"Never mind what I have to get in here," I said. "Who's Stan Waldrop?"

"He's a comedian," Stilwell said, "stand-up comic. I've seen him on Carolyn's Comedy Club, and the Improv, and I think HBO."

"The guy's that good?"

"He's funny."

"Does he make a lot of money?" Taylor asked.

"You know what your problem is?" Stilwell asked his partner. "You're greedy. That's why we're in the mess we're in, because you're greedy and everybody knows it."

"You're blamin' this on me?" Taylor asked, and that's when I walked away. The two of them bickered like a married couple most of the time, and I didn't need to hear it right now.

I walked around the bar and strolled to the back booth. The man saw me coming and stood up. He was about five eight, stocky, with his hair worn shaggy, not bad looking. Judging from the look on his face, he was far from happy, and not in the mood to crack any jokes.

"Mr. Jacoby?"

"That's right."

He extended his hand and I shook it. He had a good, strong grip, but he was no Joe Piscopo.

"I'm Stan Waldrop."

"So I've been told. Why don't you sit back down, Mr. Waldrop. Can I get you something? A beer?"

"A beer would be good," he said, sliding back into the booth.

I turned and caught Geneva's eye and she nodded. It took her half a minute to come over with two Icehouse beers. Of all the ice beers on the market so far, it is by far the smoothest. It's brewed in Milwaukee by something called Plank Brewery. The bottle claims that they were established in 1855, but I hadn't heard of them until recently.

"Ice beer," he said, studying the glass. "What will the Eskimos think of next?"

I assumed that was an attempt at a joke. He was no Robin Williams.

"What can I do for you, Mr. Waldrop?"

"Do you know me?" For a minute I thought I was in the middle of an American Express commercial.

"I'm told you're a famous comedian."

"Well, hardly famous. I work, though, more and more these days. Things are picking up, my career's on a roll, and I might be famous in a couple of years. At least, that's what I thought until . . ."

"Until what, Mr. Waldrop?"

He hesitated, then said, "Until somebody stole my jokes. Mr. Jacoby, you've got to help me get my career back."

▽

4

"YOU'RE GOING TO have to explain that to me, Mr. Waldrop."

"Stan," he said, "just call me Stan."

"All right, Stan, I'm listening."

He took a healthy swig of beer before he started talking.

"First you got to know something about me. I'm from New York, and I've been telling jokes all my life. I was the class clown in high school, you know?"

"Where'd you go to school?"

"Tilden High School, in Brooklyn."

I'd tried to get into Tilden when I was a kid. My grades held me back. Maybe Waldrop was the class clown, but he was no dummy.

I was smart enough to know that. There was a joker in every class, but few of them went on to be professional comics. In fact, they paid so little attention that few of them went on to become professional anythings.

"I wasn't a real good student, you know?" he said, as if to confirm my thoughts."

"You got into Tilden."

He waved that away.

"I was an okay student in junior high, but once I got to high school I went south. I didn't have a good enough memory to retain everything they were teaching. When I got out of high school I started working as a comic. I'd take any kind of job, parties, weddings—yeah, I did weddings—bar mitzvahs, too."

"I've never seen a comic at a wedding."

"Well, I did it. I worked odd jobs while I tried to perfect my craft. I didn't do real well in the beginning. Do you know why?"

"No, why?"

"Same reason I stunk in school. I've got no memory. I kept forgetting the jokes."

"That sounds like it would be a definite problem for a comic."

"It was, but then I got smart and I started writing them down. I mean, every time I came up with a new joke it went into a book."

"A joke book?"

"You could call it that. A joke book, a diary, whatever. A few years ago I got myself a computer and now I've got my jokes in there."

"I see."

"That is, I did have them in there."

"Did? What happened—did you, uh, what is it, delete them?" I wasn't exactly computer literate, but sometimes you just pick up the lingo.

"I didn't," he said, "but somebody sure as hell did. I went into my joke file yesterday, only it wasn't there."

"How could that happen?"

"I don't know. Either somebody got into my apartment and erased it, or somebody did it by phone."

"That can be done?"

"Sure. I've got a modem and somebody could have called in, accessed the file, copied it, and then erased it."

That much lingo lost me, but I caught the gist of what he meant.

"Why would somebody do that?"

"To steal my act!"

"Is that generally done?"

"Haven't you ever heard of Henny Youngman? He stole everybody's jokes."

"I thought that was a joke."

"Well, in my case I ain't laughing. Somebody's got my jokes, Mr. Jacoby, and I'd like to hire you to find them for me."

I didn't know if he meant the jokes or the thief, but I didn't ask. It had to be one or the other.

"Stan, what makes you think somebody has them? What if they just erased them?"

"No," Waldrop said, "I think somebody is trying to steal my jokes and ruin me. Look, I got a lousy memory, but I'm a good joke writer."

I stared at him.

"Who parted the Arctic Ocean?" he asked.

"What?"

"Who parted the Arctic Ocean?"

I caught it the second time. It was a joke.

"Who?"

"Eski-Moses."

I smiled.

"I remember that one because it's so good."

"It's funny."

"I know it's funny, and so is my other stuff. Please, Mr. Jacoby, without my jokes I'm dead."

"Can't you write some more?"

"I can, but it would take time, lots of time, and I've got a chance to do 'Comic Relief' next month, on HBO. Billy called me."

"Billy?"

"Billy Crystal. He and Robin Williams and Whoopi host 'Comic Relief'."

Whoopi could only be Whoopi Goldberg. I didn't spend a lot of time watching TV, but I knew that much. On occasion I saw a movie. Some years back I saw one called *Jumpin' Jack Flash*, and she was in it. It wasn't bad.

"I don't know if I can write a whole new act by then. I need my jokes or I'm gonna miss out on this big break."

I didn't know if I wanted any part of this. I needed a way to say no.

"Who sent you to me, Stan?"

"A friend of yours."

"Who?"

He hesitated, then said, "She asked me not to say."

"Why not?"

"She said she wanted you to take my case on merit, not because she sent me."

Whoever my friend was, she was right. If she was a good enough friend I would have felt compelled to take him on as a favor to her.

Whoever she was.

"Whataya say, Mr. Jacoby?"

"Have you heard of the new drink, the Tonya Bobbitt?"

"Club soda with a slice," he said with a grin. "Don't quit your day job."

▽

5

WE DISCUSSED MY fee. Waldrop said he wasn't rich, but that my fee wouldn't be a problem. I wanted to tell him that he caught me at just the right time. My fees were about to go up.

After I'd collected all of Waldrop's personal data—address, telephone number, hours to contact him—I asked him to give me some names and addresses of colleagues he might suspect. In addition, I got the name and address of his agent.

"Do you want to see me work?" he asked suddenly.

"Uh, sure, why not?"

"I'm appearing at a place in the Village tomorrow night. I'll leave your name at the door. It's seven P.M."

"I'll be there."

"Bring a friend. I do some stuff with the audience, and we'll have some fun." He scribbled the address of the club on a napkin.

"I'll see if I can find somebody."

He left and I went back behind the bar.

"Is he funny in person?" Stilwell asked.

"A riot."

"We gotta go," Taylor said. "We're meetin' somebody."

I got the feeling that they weren't taking their suspension lightly at all, and that they were just killing time here.

"Watch your step, guys. If you need any help, give me a call."

"Thanks, Jack," Taylor said.

"Hey," Stilwell said, "if *you* need any help, give us a call. We could use something to do."

"Sure."

As they left, Geneva turned to me. "What did the funny white dude want?"

"That's confidential, Geneva," I said. "You know that."

"I'll give you something confidential . . ."

I laughed and told her what Waldrop wanted me to do.

"You mean he's got to write everything down? What does he do, stand up on stage with a big cue card?"

"Do you want to see what he does? He invited me to his show tomorrow night."

"Oh, no," Geneva said, "I got better things to do with my time than watch some sad-looking white dude try to be funny on stage."

"Suit yourself, but you're probably going to be missing a great time."

"I'll live."

Something occurred to me then.

"Gen?"

"Yo."

"Don't we have a regular who's in show business?"

She leaned back against the cash register and thought a moment. It was a nice pose.

"I know who you mean," she said. "Guy who's always braggin' that he works in TV? Faggy-looking guy with poofed-up hair?"

"That's him. What's his name?"

"I don't know. Ask Marty when he comes in, maybe he knows." She pushed away from the register. "I don't keep track of the faggy-lookin' guys who come in here—which means I don't keep track of most of our customers."

I was trying to think of a comeback when the phone rang.

"You wanna get that?" Geneva asked.

"You're the manager."

"You the owner."

She got me there.

"Jack?"

It was Heck Delgado, a lawyer friend of mine I sometimes did some work for. He had his own investigators, but every once in a while he found some work to toss my way. In fact, he had even worked with Walker Blue once or twice. Missy, who used to be Eddie Waters's secretary, went to work for Heck after Eddie was killed. Since then I'd always wondered if the two of them hadn't started some other kind of relationship.

"Hello, Heck. What's going on?"

"Miles, could you come to my office later this afternoon?"

"Sure. What's up?"

"A job you might be interested in," Heck said. "I'll give you the details when you get here. Around three this afternoon, okay?"

"Sure, Heck, I'll be there."

As I hung up Marty showed up for work, late as usual.

"Sorry, Boss—"

"Forget it. You got here before the lunch rush, that's what counts. Hey, Marty, wait a minute."

Marty's a student at NYU and usually drops his books in the back when he arrives. Now he put them on top of the bar and turned to face me.

"Yeah, Boss?"

"There's a guy who comes in here sometimes who's pretty loud about working in TV."

"Frank Silvero."

"That's his name?"

"That's it."

"Is he on the level?"

"I think so. Either that or he talks a good game."

"What kind of work does he do?"

"I don't know for sure, but he claims he works on some sitcoms."

"If he comes in here today or tomorrow, do me a favor, will you? See if you can get me his phone number."

"You looking to break into TV?"

"I'm working on a case, and I think he might be able to help me. I just want to ask him some questions."

"He'll probably be interested in talking to you, all right," Mary said. "He thinks a PI who owns a bar might be a good idea for TV."

"Really?"

"Yeah, he thinks he could make a sitcom out of it."

"A sitcom?"

Marty shrugged and went around behind the bar. He goosed Geneva as he passed her; she took a futile swipe at him.

"I'm gonna fire his ass, he don't learn to keep his hands to himself."

Marty usually wore tight jeans to work, making him a hit with some of the women we were pulling in now that we were moving up. Idly, I wondered if he and Geneva were . . .

"Who says you can hire and fire?"

"I hired him, didn't I?"

She got me again.

"Do me a favor," I said. "Don't fire him, we need him."

"I'll break his arms, then."

"One arm," I said, "so he can still work."

"You know what's wrong with you, Boss?"

"What?"

"You let your employees walk all over you."

"I don't—"

"Now get out from behind the bar, boy, you in my way."

I got.

▽

6

Heck's office was on Fifth Avenue, at Twenty-third Street. This part of Fifth Avenue doesn't have as many flashy steel and glass high-rises as there are uptown. I often wondered why he didn't move to a new building. I knew that he was fairly successful at what he did and could afford it. As I got into the small, rickety elevator I thought again about my own recent move. Joining Walker Blue in partnership was probably the most serious attempt I'd ever made to try to improve my life and my lifestyle. Still, Walker and I did things differently. What if we didn't get along?

I stepped out of the elevator into a small entry foyer and followed an arrow with a sign to a door that said HECTOR DELGADO, ATTORNEY-AT-LAW. I opened the door and entered, and Missy looked up from her desk and smiled.

Missy had worked for Eddie Waters for a few years, and I knew for a fact that she and Eddie had had a relationship. He was older than she, and it never got anywhere near being permanent. Still, she had been devastated by his death, and it had been months later when she'd accepted Heck's offer of a job. I had tried to keep Eddie's business going, but eventually had to give up the office.

"Miles, hi! Coffee?"

I walked to the desk and gave her a brotherly peck on the cheek. We had never been in a situation where I could take a run at Missy, so I settled for a brother/sister type of relationship—well, maybe kissin' cousins, with some idle lust thrown in.

She looked good today, wearing a simple black dress with a pink linen jacket over it. She had a thick gold rope around her neck that hung too high to be a chain and too low to be a choker.

"Sounds good. Is he in?"

She handed me a mug that said TRY IT, I MIGHT LIKE IT and said, "Take your coffee and go right in. He's with a client."

I took the coffee from her—black, no sugar—and walked to Heck's door. I knocked once and then opened the door and stepped inside.

"Miles, good, I'm glad you're here."

"It's three o'clock," I said, "where else would I be?"

The other man was sitting in a chair in front of Heck's desk. He did not turn around to look at me. There was an empty chair next to him.

"I want you to meet someone." Hector Domingo Gonzales Delgado remained seated and beckoned with a wave for me to come closer.

Heck was every girl's wet dream of what a successful attorney should look like. He was tall, in his mid-thirties, and usually wore a three-piece suit that fit perfectly because he kept athletically trim with constant workouts. He had a Ricardo Montalban accent that thickened slightly when he became agitated.

Lately, however, he had taken to dressing more casually when he wasn't scheduled to go to court. Today he had on a short-sleeved green shirt with not quite red stripes—actually, it wasn't quite green, either. Jade and . . . what? I'd ask Missy on the way out, if I was still interested. Anyway, he was wearing lightweight khaki Levi's with it, and if he tossed a jacket on over it all he'd still look fairly businesslike . . . for spring.

"This is Truman Tyler, Miles. Truman, Miles Jacoby, the detective I was telling you about."

"Investigator," I said. "Detective" is a police rank in New York City.

"Ah, yes," Heck said.

I walked around to where I could see Tyler better. He hadn't made a good impression on me by not moving when I'd entered the room. Now he looked up and managed to look down his nose while he was at it. Even seated I could see that he was six feet. He appeared to be in his early forties, with Dustin Hoffman's jaw and nose and a hairline that was both receding and turning gray. I wondered which would win. His suit was nowhere near Heck's standards, and even made me feel overdressed in the sports jacket I'd bought from a little Village men's shop.

"Mr. Tyler."

"Have a seat, Miles," Heck said.

"That's okay."

I wanted to be standing, watching Tyler's face, not sitting next to him. He made me uncomfortable, like I had an army of ants underneath my clothes, and I didn't know why.

"All right," Heck said, sitting back and eyeing me for a moment. "Mr. Tyler called me earlier today and asked to meet with me. He also asked that I try to have you here."

"Why me?" I directed my question to Tyler, not Heck.

"I have a client who is in the Tombs right now," Tyler said. "He has been arrested for murder and is awaiting arraignment."

I sipped my coffee and waited.

"He says he knows both of you."

"Does this client have a name?"

Tyler nodded. "Danny Pesce."

"Don't tell me, let me guess. They called him 'Danny the Fish'?"

Tyler frowned and said, "That's right."

"And why would Danny the Fish send you to see me and Heck?"

"Because his alibi is somebody you know very well. We'd like you to try and find him."

"Somebody I know? Who?"

I looked at Tyler, then at Heck, then back to Tyler.

"A man named Raymond Carbone."

"Ray?" I looked at Heck. He knew Ray Carbone because he'd met him through me. Like myself, Ray was an ex-fighter, but while I had gone legit with a PI license, Ray did some strong-arm work, some bodyguard work, and some occasional work for me.

"What's Ray got to do with your client?"

"Like I said, my client claims that Mr. Carbone can alibi him for the time of the murder."

"Then why don't you ask him?"

"I went to Mr. Carbone's residence, but he wasn't there. I asked his neighbors where he was, but they haven't seen him in days."

"So you think Ray ran out? He wouldn't do that."

"I am not saying he did," Tyler said, "I just want you to find him."

I looked at Heck.

"What's your part in this?"

"Apparently," Heck said, "Mr. Pesce would like me to defend him."

"I thought you were his lawyer?" I said, looking at Tyler.

"Yes, well, I have been his attorney for some, uh, lesser offenses, but since this is a murder charge, Mr. Pesce asked me to approach Mr. Delgado."

I looked at Heck.

"When I heard that they were looking for Ray Carbone, I figured you'd want in."

"Working for you?"

"Naturally."

I hesitated a moment, then turned to face Heck fully.

"Why don't we let Mr. Tyler get on with his day and you and I can discuss this?"

"Mr. Tyler," Heck said, after just the slightest hesitation, "I will get back to you later today."

Tyler looked from Heck to me, then back to Heck, probably wondering who was calling the shots.

"Well," he said finally, standing up, "I'll wait for your call." He was looking at Heck when he said it.

Heck was looking at me expectantly.

7

I WAITED UNTIL Tyler had left the office and then sat in the chair next to the one he'd vacated. I reached for Heck's phone and dialed Ray Carbone's home number. After it had rung ten times I hung up. There was one other number I had for Ray. I tried it, with the same result.

"Carbone?"

I nodded. "No answer. Heck, what's your take on this?"

"What do you mean?"

"Why does this guy Pesce want you?"

Heck shrugged and said, "Because I'm good."

"What do you know about Tyler?"

"I've seen him around the courthouse," Heck said. "His clients are less than desirable. Let me ask you something."

"Okay."

"Would Ray Carbone be involved with someone like Danny Pesce?"

"I don't know that I can answer that, since I don't know what type of person Danny Pesce is."

Heck gave me a couple of raised eyebrows and said, "Danny the Fish?"

"Okay, Ray's in with some made guys. He works both sides of the fence."

"So he could be involved in a murder?"

"Anybody could be involved in a murder, but Tyler didn't say he was involved. He said he could alibi his client."

"And maybe he can."

"Are you taking this case?"

"I'm going to the Tombs tomorrow to talk with Mr. Pesce. Do you want to come?"

I thought it over, then shook my head.

"No, I'll leave it to you to talk to the guy. I'll get started on trying to find Ray. Whether you take the case or not, I want to find out if anything's happened to him."

"If I take the case," Heck said, "you'll be on the clock."

"Naturally."

"Will this be your case alone," he asked, "or yours and Walker's?"

"What do you know about me and Walker?"

"I know he called me to see if I thought you'd be interested in a partnership."

"And what did you tell him?"

"I told him that I'd be honored if you would come in with me."

"Partners with *you*?"

Heck cleared his throat. "I'm not asking, mind you. I, uh, like working alone."

"I do too," I said, "it's just getting harder and harder to afford."

"So?"

"So am I going partners with Walker?"

"Yes."

"I am."

Heck smiled, and I could just imagine rows of women swooning. "Congratulations. I think it's a good move, for both of you."

"Did you know about Walker's heart?"

"I had heard something, but I never asked. I thought if he wanted me to know he would have called."

"It's funny."

"What is?"

"I haven't had a case in weeks, and now that I've agreed to go partners with Walker I got two today."

"Two?"

I told him briefly about Stan Waldrop.

"And who referred him?"

"He didn't say."

"Any ideas?"

"None," I said, "but maybe I'll find out later, after I tell him I'll take his case."

"And are you taking it?"

"I guess so. Maybe I need just one last solo fling."

Heck laughed. "It is an odd pairing, isn't it?"

I thought about pretending to be insulted, but instead I said, "Yeah, I guess it is."

Heck shuffled some papers on his desk. Time to get back to business.

"I'll call Mr. Tyler tonight and tell him that you are at least putting in some hours today looking for Ray Carbone, pending what happens when I interview Mr. Pesce."

"When are you seeing him?"

"Nine A.M. tomorrow."

"I'll call here at noon and check in with you."

"Fine. I'll probably be having lunch at my desk. It is fast becoming a way of life."

I left his office and stopped by Missy's on the way out.

"I heard about you and Walker, Miles. Have you agreed?"

"I have."

"That's wonderful," she said, putting her hand on my arm and squeezing. "Eddie would be pleased. He always had the highest regard for Walker Blue."

It was odd, but her words about Eddie filled me with a warmth I wasn't prepared for.

"Heck's looking sharp these days. Are you getting him to dress more casually?"

"I admit it's my influence," she said, blushing slightly.

"That's a great shirt he's wearing—what is it, green and what?"

"Jade and fuchsia."

"Fuchsia?"

She nodded.

"I could make some suggestions for you too, Miles."

"What's wrong with the way I dress?"

"You're not a boxer anymore. Also, if you're going to be partners with Walker Blue . . ."

"I'll see you soon, Missy."

"I'll make some notes—" she was shouting as I ran out the door.

8

Ray Carbone lived in an apartment building in Alphabet City. He could probably have afforded better, but Ray was the kind of guy who felt more comfortable living in a dangerous environment. Of course, no neighborhood seems as dangerous to its residents as it does to outsiders.

Ray's apartment was on Thirteenth Street between Avenues A and B. The building was an old five-story brownstone, and Ray had one of the two fifth-floor apartments. I tried his doorbell in front, and when there was no answer I decided to try his back door.

Well, not a back door, but he did have a fire escape that he sometimes used as an emergency entrance. Or exit. I had to stand on a garbage can to reach the ladder and pull it down.

Going up the fire escape past four other apartments, it's kind of hard not to sneak a peek. Two of them seemed empty. On the second floor a man was sitting in a chair with a can of beer, probably watching a television.

On the fourth floor, just below Ray's place, a man and a woman were on a bed and they weren't sleeping. I stared a few seconds longer than I had to and then went up to the next level feeling embarrassed. If I wanted to see that sort of thing I could rent a skin flick.

When I reached Ray's window I tried it and found it locked. I peered inside. The bed was unmade, and on the nightstand were two beer cans. I knew Ray had installed an unseen catch somewhere on top of the window, which would enable him to spring the lock from the outside. If a would-be burglar didn't know it was there, he'd have a hard time getting the window open, as Ray had installed a magnetic lock system.

I felt around on top of the window but couldn't find anything. Next I tried the window frame and felt something. It wasn't a catch, or a button. It felt like a piece of metal. I ran my hand up the other side and there was another one.

I looked through my pockets for something metal and came up with my key ring. I picked the thickest key and took it off the ring, then held it against one of the pieces of metal. It must have broken some kind of magnetic seal, because I heard a snap as the lock clicked. I put my keys away, tried the window and found it unlocked. I opened it as quietly as I could. I crawled inside, closing the window behind me.

Once in I was hit with the musty smell apartments get when they've been closed up for days. A quick search of the three rooms established that Ray hadn't been here for a while. There were dishes in the sink and take-out cartons on the counter. I looked through the garbage and came out with two delivery receipts, one for pizza and one for Chinese. Both had dates on them. One was from four days before, and the other three.

I looked in the refrigerator and found three cans of beer, a container of orange juice that was just about empty, and a spoiled container of milk. In the freezer were half a dozen frozen dinners and a half-filled container of Rocky Road ice cream. I didn't know Ray had a sweet tooth, but then we really didn't hang out together much.

In the living room there were some *Ring* magazines scattered about, and a couple of other sports magazines. The *Sports Illustrated* swimsuit issue was on the sofa, facedown and open. I picked it up and looked at it. Kathy Ireland was looking as good as ever. I went through the room quickly, and then did the same with the bedroom. I didn't know what I was looking for, and I didn't find anything.

I left the bathroom for last, just on the off chance that Ray was in the tub. He wasn't.

I went back to the living room and sat down next to his phone. He had an answering machine, and a blinking red light indicated that there were six messages.

The first and third messages were from Truman Tyler, saying that he really needed to speak to Ray as soon as possible.

The second message was from Ray's girl, Joy, just an "I-miss-you-call-me-honey" type of message.

The fourth message was a hang-up.

The fifth message was the one I found most interesting. Nobody spoke after the beep, but there were two distinct beeps following the one meant to record after. They were the kind of beeps I hear on mine when I've checked messages from outside. That meant that Ray was alive enough, maybe within the past day, to have checked his messages.

It wasn't until then that I realized I was afraid he was dead.

The sixth message was from a bill collector. Apparently Ray was behind on his Visa payments.

Once I'd listened to the messages, the light stopped blinking. I knew if I pressed the "save" button, the light would start blinking again. If Ray came home and saw that, he'd never know someone had listened. I was afraid Ray wasn't coming home soon, though, so I wasn't worried. In fact, as a last thought I took the tape out of the machine and put it in my pocket.

Satisfied that I'd given the apartment a thorough enough going-over, I left by the front door; it would lock behind me. Maybe the window would have locked behind me, but I wanted to talk to some of the other tenants before I left the building. I was hoping someone had seen Ray in the past day or two. It occurred to me then that I knew when Danny Pesce had been arrested, but I didn't know when he was supposed to have committed the murder. I was going to have to get that information from Heck if I was going to talk to Ray about it.

When I found him.

9

I STARTED DOWN the stairs and stopped at the door of the apartment directly beneath Ray's. I was about to knock to ask the couple if they'd seen him recently. Considering what I had seen them doing through the window, I decided not to. They wouldn't be very receptive at the moment to my questions.

I tried the other apartment on the fourth floor, then the two on the third. No one was home. It was only about three in the afternoon, and they were probably still at work.

I went to the second floor, where I knew at least one of the apartments was occupied because I had seen the guy watching TV.

When he answered my knock, I asked him if he had seen Ray Carbone around.

"Who?"

"One of the tenants on the fifth floor?" I pointed up so he'd get the idea. "Carbone?"

He was a Hispanic man in his fifties, wearing a tank-top T-shirt and badly in need of some deodorant.

"I ain' seen nobody."

"Do you know Ray?"

"I don' know nobody."

"Is your neighbor across the hall home, do you think?"

"Her? She's almost always home . . . and available, if you know what I mean." He wriggled his eyebrows.

"I think I know what you mean," I said. "She's good for some action, huh?"

"All kinds of action."

"You, uh, getting any of it?"

"Sure," he said. "I get it when I want it. She loves havin' me come over there."

"What about her and Ray?"

He frowned.

"I tol' you, I don' know no Ray."

"Maybe you can tell me—"

"I don' know nothin'!"

"Look, I'm not a cop."

"Good," he said, "me neither," and closed the door in my face.

I'd had to breathe in his b.o. and had nothing to show for it.

I went across the hall and knocked on that door. I was willing to take what he'd just told me about the tenant with a grain of salt.

When she opened the door, I could at least believe that she liked some action. She was about five seven, a big girl with heavy breasts inside a tank-top T-shirt that hid very little. She had dark hair that was rather lank at the moment. She was holding a beer can in a hand with a cigarette between the first and second fingers. She looked to be in her mid-thirties, with some crinkle lines around her eyes. Her mouth was puffy, and I wasn't sure if she had thick lips or if she'd been hit lately. Also, the way women are injecting stuff in their lips these days, who knew? It did give her a sort of overblown sexy look, though.

"Whataya want?"

"I'm looking for Ray Carbone, one of your neighbors."

"You a cop?"

"No, I'm not a cop. I'm a friend of Ray's, and I'm worried about him. Nobody's seen him for a few days."

"Ray can take care of himself."

"I know he can. Can you just tell me if you've seen him?"

"Naw," she said, "I ain't seen him since—well, since the last time he was here."

"Here? In his apartment, or do you mean yours?"

"Here, right here in my place."

"Does Ray come down here a lot?"

She gave me a slow smile and leaned her hips against the door. She was wearing a pair of faded jeans and filled them to bursting.

"Yeah, he comes down once in a while. We got it on, ya know?"

"Yeah, I know."

Suddenly she stood straight up and asked, "Did you talk to the asshole across the hall?"

"Your neighbor? Yeah, I talked to him."

"What'd that sonofabitch tell you about me?"

I answered her truthfully. What did I owe the guy after he'd slammed his door in my face?

"He told me that you and him get it on a lot."

"That scumbag? I wouldn't let him lick my vibrator. Hey, Martinez, you lying asshole!" she shouted, taking one step into the hall. "Come out here."

Martinez was apparently not as dumb as he'd looked. He stayed where he was. I think if he had come out she would have hurt him. She had a couple of inches and about twenty pounds on him.

"When was that last time you saw Ray?"

"I dunno," she said, still snarling at her neighbor's closed door. "Few days ago."

"Two days? Three?"

"Naw . . . I think it was four days ago. Yeah, it was Sunday, 'cause I didn't have to—I mean, I was home."

"Are you home a lot?"

She took her eyes from the door across the hall and looked at me again.

"Are you sure you're not a cop?"

"I'm sure."

"Well, yeah, I'm home a lot. I work at home . . . sometimes . . . ya know?"

"Yeah, I know."

"Hey," she said, cocking her hip again, "wanna come inside for a while?"

"Sorry," I said, "but I've really got to find Ray. Thanks for the offer, though."

"What offer? You think I was offerin' you a freebie? I only do freebies for my friends."

"Like Ray?"

"Yeah, like Ray. What's it to ya?"

"Nothing," I said, "nothing at all. Thanks for talking to me."

"Get fucked!" she said, and slammed the door.

Not today.

I went back up to the fourth floor and knocked on the apartment door I hadn't tried yet. Maybe they'd finished doing what they'd been doing.

Then again, maybe they hadn't.

Nobody answered.

I put my ear to the door, but I didn't hear anything. They couldn't have gotten past me on the stairs. Maybe they had finished and fallen asleep; I doubted they'd finished, dressed, and left while I was in Ray's apartment. I knocked again, louder this time, but there was still no answer.

I'd have to make a point to come back and try again. I left the building figuring my next step was to check with Ray's girlfriend, Joy.

10

JOY WHITE LIVED in a brownstone on Horatio Street just west of Ninth Avenue, similar to the one Ray lived in. Technically speaking, the area is the West Village, although most of what's happening in the Village—the shops, the bookstores, the clubs, the funky bars, and the galleries—are south of there.

I'd met Joy several times. She was a bleached blond who sometimes dressed as if she belonged in the sixties. There were times when she wore tight pants and sweaters, and although she certainly had the body for them, they'd looked more timely when they'd been worn by Jayne Mansfield. Also, I often wondered about Joy—as I have wondered about many other women—why when they bleach their hair blond they leave their eyebrows dark. In addition, she wore so much makeup you almost couldn't tell that she was pretty underneath it all.

I'd accompanied Ray to Joy's apartment once, and that being the only time I'd been there—at night, in a cab— when I reached Horatio Street this time, on foot, I had to walk up and down the block twice before identifying her building.

Joy worked as an aerobics instructor in a small gym in the Village, and Ray said her hours were her own because she was so good at it. I found her doorbell beneath her mailbox and pressed it once.

"Who is it?"

"Joy, it's Miles Jacoby."

There was a moment when I thought she wasn't going to let me in, but then she buzzed me in.

She was on the second floor, and as I remembered, she had the front apartment overlooking the street. When I knocked on her door, I heard at least three locks snap open. She cracked the door as far as the chain would allow, then slammed it when she saw me, removed the chain, and opened it again.

"Miles?"

She recognized me, but the question in her voice had to do with why I was here. Why would her boyfriend's friend be showing up at her door in the middle of the day?

"Hi, Joy."

"What are you doing here?"

I tried to look past her into the apartment, but there wasn't much to see from this vantage point.

She stood in the doorway, looking better than I'd ever seen her. Her hair was pulled back in a long ponytail, and she was wearing a sweatshirt and sweatpants. I knew that underneath the baggy clothes she had an aerobic instructor's body, and I liked her dressed this way better than when she wore skintight clothes.

I was surprised, too, at how young and soft she looked without all the makeup. The woman I'd talked to in Ray's building had been sexy in a slutty, slumming sort of way. Joy, however, exuded pure sex appeal in waves—even though she dressed it wrong sometimes—and I wondered what Ray would be doing with the semi-pro who lived in his building when he could be here.

"I'm looking for Ray, Joy. Is he here?"

"No, he's not. In fact, I left a message on his answering machine earlier this week. I haven't seen him in a few days."

I knew that because I had the tape with her voice on it in my pocket.

"I'm getting worried."

"Can I come in, Joy?"

"Sure," she said, and backed away to let me enter. She

closed the door behind us and engaged all the locks. Now we were standing in the kitchen.

"Is Ray in trouble, Miles?"

"He might be if I don't find him."

"What kind of trouble?"

"Joy, do you know what kind of work Ray does?"

"Sure," she said, "I know he . . . does favors for people sometimes. I know he's not always, you know, on the up-and-up."

"Well, then, that's the kind of trouble he might be in. The kind you can get into doing the kind of work he does."

"Is Ray dead, Miles?" She held her breath after the question.

"No, Joy, Ray's not dead."

"If he was, would you tell me?"

"Yes, I would."

She studied me for a moment, then said, "Okay. Do you want a beer? I was just doing some exercises."

On the floor in the living room I could see a step, the kind they used for step aerobics. Also, there was some music on the stereo that she must have turned down when she answered the door. Now that I was inside I could smell her. It was a mixture of her perfume and her sweat.

"No, no beer, thanks," I said. "I just want to ask you some questions."

"All right."

"Are you sure you haven't seen Ray in a few days?"

"Positive."

"Have you heard from him?"

"No. Like I told you, I left a message on his machine. You could check."

"I will," I said, so she wouldn't know I already had.

"The last time you saw him, how was he?"

"He was fine. He spent the night here—it was Sunday night, I think. He left Monday morning and said he'd call me. He still hasn't."

Today was Thursday. Sunday was also the day the woman

in Ray's building had said he'd spent time with her. Either Ray slept with both women on the same day, or one of them was lying.

"Did he say what he'd be doing Monday?"

"He didn't—wait a minute."

"What?"

"Before he left he called his own phone, you know, to check messages?"

"And?"

"When he hung up, he said he had to go see somebody."

"That day? Monday?"

"Yes."

"Joy, when did you leave your message?"

"Monday night, when I didn't hear from him."

So the messages on the tape I had were from Monday on.

"Have you been to his apartment?"

She made a face.

"No, he knows I hate it there, that's why he always comes here. I want him to move out of there."

"I don't blame you."

"I want him to move in here."

"How does he feel about that?"

"Oh, you know," she said with a shrug. "He doesn't want to lose his freedom."

"Look, Joy, this is important. If you hear from him, will you do two things for me?"

"Sure. What?"

"Number one, tell him I'm looking for him and second, call me right away."

"Okay."

"Listen to me. If he's in trouble, he's going to want to handle it himself. He'll tell you not to call me, but you have to do it anyway. Understand?"

"But if he tells me not to—"

"Tell him you won't, and then do it."

"Lie to Ray?"

"Joy? You've never lied to a man?"

"Oh sure," she said, and then added, "but not to Ray."

I took hold of her shoulders and said, "This is about murder, Joy. You've got to call me if you hear from him."

She bit her lip and then nodded shortly.

"Okay, Miles, I'll call you."

"Thanks."

She opened the door for me and leaned on it. "Ray says you're one of his very best friends."

"I am, Joy," I said, "that's why I'm trying to help him."

"Will you call me when you know something?"

"First thing," I said. "I promise."

She closed the door behind me, and I heard the locks snap into place. I thought I had made an impression on her as to the importance of calling me. I only hoped that if she did hear from Ray, he didn't make a better one against me.

▽

11

Between going to Heck's office, and then to Ray's place, and then Joy's, it felt like a long day. From Joy's apartment it was a healthy walk to Packy's. When I entered, I was pleased to see that we were doing a brisk business. Marty and Ed were behind the bar, and Geneva was waiting tables. Usually whichever one of us was free waited tables, because I was still resisting hiring a full-time waitress. I thought again about how being partners with Walker Blue could save me from having to make those kinds of decisions.

"Hi, Boss." Geneva greeted me with a big grin.

"Nice crowd."

"Yeah, and everything seems to be flowing real smooth."

Which meant there were no demanding customers making it hard on her.

"Need some help?"

"No, not unless you feel like it."

"I'm going to go into the office for a while. If it gets bad and you need me, come and get me."

"You got it."

I went in the back and sat down at my desk. It had been Packy's desk, and if I hadn't had the top completely covered with ledgers, bills, newspapers, and other junk, I would have been able to see the scarred, pitted surface. It was over fifty years old and had tons of character. It deserved to be sanded and refinished, but if I'd tried to do that sort of work I would have hurt myself.

I was tempted to call Heck, but he wouldn't have the

answers to a lot of my questions until he saw Danny Pesce. I wondered if I should call Walker and tell him that I had taken on two new cases, but we weren't really partners yet—not unless some papers had come from a lawyer while I was gone. I skimmed the very top of the mess on my desk and there were no legal papers in sight, so no, we weren't partners, yet.

I thought about Stan Waldrop then. I felt guilty that I hadn't done any work on his problem. Before he'd left, along with his personal info, I had gotten the names of some of his fellow comedians who he thought might be behind the loss of his material. I wasn't sure how I was going to proceed. What would I do—see them and ask if they had stolen his act?

I decided that the first thing I should do was go and talk to his agent tomorrow. Maybe the guy would tell me that Waldrop was paranoid and was always accusing people of stealing his jokes.

I took out the notebook I'd written everything in, a little spiral job I keep in one pocket or the other. I was about to go through it when there was a knock on the door and Marty stuck his head in.

"Hey, Boss?"

"Yeah, Marty?" I wondered what we were short of now. Vermouth?

"You know that fella you asked me about earlier today?"

"What fella—oh yeah, the sitcom guy."

"He's outside, sitting at the bar. You wanna talk to him?"

I thought a moment. Could he really help me? But where was the harm in just talking to the guy?

"Yeah, I do, Marty. Thanks."

I followed him back out to the bar and he pointed the guy out. He was a typical yuppie, wearing a short-sleeved pullover shirt with a little pony or something on the chest. Now that I saw him, I realized that I knew him on sight. He usually came in for lunch, dressed in a suit. I didn't know he came by in the evenings, though.

He was talking to two other guys, so I didn't hesitate to interrupt him. They were either talking about women or sports.

"Excuse me, Frank Silvero?"

He turned his head and looked across the bar at me.

"Hey, Jack, right?"

"That's right."

"H-e-e-e-y," he drawled, putting his hand out. As he pumped my hand enthusiastically he said to the other two, "This is Kid Jacoby, guys. He owns this place, and he used to be a promising middleweight."

"I don't know how promising I was," I said, but the other two weren't listening. Maybe they'd seen me fight.

"Frank, can I talk to you a minute?"

"Sure, Jack, sure," he said, as if we'd known each other forever. "Excuse me, guys."

We moved to the far end of the bar where we could speak a little more privately.

"Frank, I understand you work in TV."

"Hey," he said, holding his hands up, palms out, "you're not gonna tell me you wanna be on TV, are you, Jack? I mean, I know George Foreman got his own show, but you know how that turned out."

"No, no," I said. "I don't want to be on TV. In fact, I have another, uh, profession. I'm a private investigator."

He paused a moment, something clicking in his head, and then he said, "I knew that. I knew that, I did."

"I was wondering if you could help me with something."

"You working on a case I can help with?"

"Maybe I am, and maybe you can. What can you tell me about stand-up comics?"

He made a face and said, "They make lousy actors. I mean, once in a while one makes good, like Eddie Murphy. But have you seen Seinfeld? The guy can't act. Paul Reiser, now he's pretty good, and he's got that Helen Hunt to work with—man, is she cute or what—but if you ever saw Frank Gorshin and Don Rickles try to act—"

"Frank, Frank," I said, getting him to put on the brakes. "I'm more interested in them as stand-ups, not as actors."

I wondered how high up this guy was where he worked. I mean, when he had to stop and switch gears I could see it on his face.

"Well, whataya want to know?"

"Their jokes, do they write them down?"

He thought a moment, then said, "I dunno."

"Well, how much joke stealing goes on among them?"

"Hey, plenty. Haven't you ever heard of Henny Youngman?"

I stared at him for a moment, then decided to cut my losses.

"Okay, thanks, Frank. You've been a big help."

"Hey, Jack, you know, if you ever do wanna get on TV I think this bit, you know, the private eye bit with the bar, I think that'd work well for a sitcom."

"I'll keep it in mind, Frank."

"I'm serious, babe," he said. "We should have lunch on it."

"I'll have my girl call your girl," I said, and fled to my office.

▽

12

I HAVE ONE answering machine, and I used to keep it in my apartment, but when I started using the office at Packy's for my PI business I moved it there. I took Ray's message tape out of my pocket and put it in my machine, then pressed the "save" button. Immediately, the little red light started to blink. Luckily, mine worked the same way Ray's did.

I played back all the messages. Joy said she had called Ray on Monday night. Hers was the second message. Tyler had probably called Ray on Monday and again on Tuesday before calling Heck. Why would he have tried Ray at all? Hadn't his client told him to go to Heck Delgado to get him for his defense? At the same time, Tyler was asking Heck—and me—to find Ray, but he obviously had Ray's phone number before he came to us. Did he have his address as well?

Not only was I going to have to talk to Heck tomorrow, but Tyler as well—and Stan Waldrop's agent, a man named John Healy.

I was playing Ray's messages back again when Geneva came in to get a bottle of gin off the shelves that lined the walls. We had enough liquor on those shelves to get an elephant drunk, and we still managed to run short of something every night.

"What are you doing? Playing with your machine?"

"I want to hear the messages on this tape over and over."

"Working on a case?"

"Yes."

"That comic guy that was here?"

"No, this is something else."

She came over, put the bottle down on the desk, and leaned on it.

"I've got the last six messages that were left on the machine, and something doesn't strike me as right. I wish I could hear what was on here before."

"You can."

I looked up at her.

"What do you mean? Once you listen to your messages, the machine tapes over them . . . doesn't it?"

"Sometimes," she said, "but you know what I found out? That tape that fits in the phone?"

"Yeah."

"It also fits into one of those microrecorders. You know, those little jobbies that fit in your pocket or, in my case, my purse."

"So?"

"So when you do that you can play all the messages that are on the tape, not just the last ones that were left on a particular day."

"And the others haven't been recorded over?"

"Some have, some haven't. Try it. I was playing around once, and there was still a message somewhere on the tape that I'd gotten weeks before."

"Geneva, is this on the level?"

She picked up the gin bottle. "Why would I lie?"

"Do you still have one of those little recorders?"

"Sure I do."

"In your purse?"

"No, I don't carry it with me everywhere I go. Get real."

"Can you bring it with you to work tomorrow? It would really help me."

Her eyes got a crafty look and she said, "For another day off with pay I can."

Lately Geneva had started to bargain for what she wanted, usually time off with pay.

"Half a day and it's a deal."

"Done. Hah! I got me a half day off."

"When we're not busy."

She made a face at me and said, "I knew there was a catch. I'll have the recorder here tomorrow, Boss."

She left, swishing her butt at me saucily like she knew she'd gotten away with something.

Before closing up and leaving the bar that night, I tried Ray's phone number. His machine didn't answer, and that's when I realized that I hadn't replaced the tape I'd taken. There was no way he could get any more messages, but more messages might help me find him. I needed to go back and put a clean tape in the machine. I'd call Joy in the morning to see if she had a key to his place so I wouldn't have to go up the fire escape again.

I left the bar and went home to my apartment on University Place and Thirteenth Street. I liked it because it was near the subway—the Fourteenth and Union Square Station—as well as being over a restaurant and across the street from a deli. I figured to stay there even when I started making more money working with Walker.

I took a beer out of the fridge—a John Courage, which I didn't carry in the bar—and went to the phone. I tried Ray again, just in case he'd come home, but hung up after four rings.

I made a quick ham sandwich for dinner, finished off the beer, and decided to turn in early. I had a busy day ahead. I was going to be talking with a lot of people, and it usually helped to be alert.

▽

13

Aғᴛᴇʀ ʙʀᴇᴀᴋFᴀsᴛ I dialed the phone number of Stan
Waldrop's agent, John Healy. What I would have liked to
have done was call Heck Delgado, but I knew he'd still be at
the Tombs talking to his—our—potential client, Danny
"the Fish" Pesce.

The phone was answered by a secretary who said that Mr.
Healy was "very busy."

"Would you tell him please that I'm calling regarding one
of his clients, Stan Waldrop?"

"And who shall I say you are, sir?" The woman sounded
young, with a deep, sexy voice.

"My name is Miles Jacoby," I said, and then added, "I'm
a detective."

"Oh, just one moment, please."

It was more like three, but who was counting?

"Hello, hello! What's this about Stan Waldrop? Did
something happen to him?"

"Mr. Healy?"

"That's correct."

"My name is Miles Jacoby."

"Detective Jacoby?"

"Um, I'm a private investigator—"

"You told my secretary you were a policeman."

"I'm sorry, sir, I did not. I told her my name, and that I
was a detective."

"I see. Well, what's this about, Mr. Jacoby?"

"Stan Waldrop."

"What about him?"

"Well, he's hired me to find some missing jokes."

"What?"

"He says somebody stole his jokes—"

"I can see this is going to take a while," Healy said, interrupting me.

"Why don't we make an appointment?"

"All right . . . wait . . . let me check . . . can you come and see me . . . between four and four-fifteen today?"

"Four and four-fifteen? Can you spare the time?"

"Yes, I can," he said impatiently, "fifteen minutes between four and four-fifteen."

"I don't suppose—" I started, but I was speaking to a dead phone.

At least I'd been granted a fifteen-minute audience. That was something.

When I got off the phone with Healy it was eleven A.M. I wanted to make a call to California, but it was too early. The man I wanted to call, a PI named Saxon, would bite my head off for sure if I called him at eight in the morning. I decided to wait until about one, my time.

Saxon was a PI whose name was in a book I had inherited from Eddie Waters, a phone book containing numbers of other PIs around the country. When he needed something done in another state, he called one of them. I had taken to doing the same thing, with great success. They say cops are a close-knit bunch, but I haven't found too many people I find nicer and more helpful than some of my colleagues.

So I'd give Saxon a call later, and I knew he'd help me if he could.

I left my apartment at eleven-thirty and walked over to Packy's. Geneva was already there, everything ready to open by noon.

"I got your recorder, Boss," she shouted as I used my key to enter.

"How about a 'good morning'?"

She put her hands on her hips and faced me. She was wearing some kind of sleeveless, hooded sweatshirt in white, with a flash of something red underneath.

"You wouldn't be here before opening if it wasn't for that recorder."

"Hey, I come in a lot before opening."

"Yeah, bite me," she said. "The recorder's on your desk."

I bit back a sexist remark about where I'd like to bite her and went into the office, stopping in the kitchen to grab a cup of Geneva's great coffee.

I sat at my desk and took the tape out of my pocket. Geneva's recorder was on the desk, looking very tiny, but the tape was a perfect fit. I put it in, rewound it to the beginning, and then pressed the "play" button.

Geneva was right. There were messages on there other than those recorded that last day. Some were just snatches, because they were constantly being recorded over, but some were there in their entirety.

As it turned out, Ray got lots of cryptic messages, probably because of the nature of his business.

"Ray, Ken, call me."

"Ray it's me. Call me tonight."

"Hey, Ray, goin' to the track Saturday. Call if you're interested."

"Ray, baby, I miss you. Call me." That was Joy. The others were male voices I didn't recognize.

And then there were the snatches:

"Mr. Carbone, please call me at . . ."

". . . one last time, and then I'm not callin' . . ."

". . . how about Tuesday . . ."

". . . heard from you in a week . . ."

". . . please hang up and dial again . . ."

". . . press 'one' to accept . . ."

All in all, there wasn't much I could use, but I was willing to listen to it a few more times just to make sure. I was rewinding it when the phone rang. I looked at the clock on my desk as I answered it. It was twelve-fifteen.

"Hello?"

"Jack?"

"Heck, are you back from the Tombs already?"

"I have what I need."

"Are you taking the case?"

"I am."

"Then I guess I am too."

"Have you found Mr. Carbone?"

"Not yet. Can we talk? I need more info."

"I'm due in court . . . wait . . . can you be here at four-thirty?"

"Maybe five. Is that okay?"

"Any time after five is fine, Miles."

"I'll see you then."

"Okay."

"Hey, you want to go and see a stand-up comic tonight?"

"A comic?"

"Yeah, I've got a client who does stand-up. He's at this place in the Village, and he's leaving two tickets for me."

"Uh, I don't think so, but thanks for the offer."

"That's okay," I said. "Be a shame to waste that other ticket."

"You'll find somebody," he said. "You're a popular guy, Miles."

Yeah, I thought as I hung up, tell that to my private life. I touched the little phone book in my pocket and thought that maybe I should ask one of my fellow PIs to go with me.

Nah!

14

LINDA MATELLA WAS a lady cop I'd met a while back while working a case. Since then we've gone out a few times, but we haven't gotten serious. She'd been involved with a married colleague whose murder I was looking into. His name was Andy McWilliams, and it was his wife, Caroline, I was helping. She also had a PI's license, and once she and I found out who had her husband killed, she tried to continue his business. We saw each other once in a while, but eventually it got to be too much for her. She packed it in and moved to the Midwest to be near her family. I never told Caroline about Linda—not that she had been seeing her husband, and not that I was seeing both of them at the same time. Even though I was seeing them casually, I still had some guilt about it. It was funny, though; Linda knew about Caroline.

Linda also knew about my long-distance relationship with Cathy Merrill, the Florida deputy.

Linda was smart, fun to be with, and somebody I think I was really resisting getting involved with—or maybe she was resisting me. Anyway, we had an occasional dinner together, and when one of us got tickets for something, invited the other one.

I called her at police headquarters, where she worked. When I got her on the phone she only had a minute, so I invited her to see Stan Waldrop with me and she accepted. We arranged for me to pick her up, and then she went back to work.

I called Joy White at home, but there was no answer. It looked like I was going to have to get into Ray's apartment the same way I had before. On the way over I stopped in an electronics store and bought some more tapes for the answering machine. The smallest pack they had was four, but I could eventually use the other three.

When I got to Ray's building, I went through the routine with the fire escape. This time, all of the apartments I passed seemed to be empty. In fact, the fourth floor apartment where I had seen the man and woman in bed looked odd. Either they were real clean people, or the apartment was vacant.

I bypassed Ray's magnetic lock again and entered his apartment. Everything looked just the way I had left it, so apparently Ray hadn't come home last night. I didn't bother with another search of the apartment; I just put the new tape in his machine. I was about to leave when I realized that there had to be an outgoing message on it.

I couldn't impersonate his voice, so I just said, "Leave a message after the tone." I vacillated over using tone or beep, and decided tone sounded better. Even if it was really a "beep," who was going to complain?

Also, when I picked up his machine and looked at the bottom there was the code number for picking up messages from outside. It was only two digits, so even I could memorize it.

I left the apartment by the front door again and stopped at the fourth floor. I knocked on the door of the apartment under Ray's. Still no answer. Then I heard somebody coming up the steps. A middle-aged woman with gray hair appeared and was so startled by my presence that she almost dropped her bag of groceries.

"Sorry if I scared you," I said.

"That's all right," she said. "I just didn't expect you." She was wearing a nurse's uniform, right down to the white shoes. "Do you want to see that apartment?"

"I'm sorry?"

"The apartment?"

"Oh, I guess there's nobody home."

She laughed and said, "Of course there's nobody home. It's vacant."

"Vacant?"

At her door she used one hand to fit her key into the lock.

"Aren't you here to see it?"

"Uh . . . if I was here to see it, who would I see?"

"Why, the super."

"And who would that be?"

"Ray Carbone."

That surprised me. Another little job for Ray. He probably got his rent taken care of that way.

"Is he around?"

"He lives up in Five B," she said, opening her door, "but I haven't seen him in days."

"I see. Uh, how long has this apartment been vacant?"

"Months," she said, then added, "maybe I shouldn't have said that. I mean, there's nothing wrong with it or anything."

"That's okay. Uh, do you want some help with those groceries?"

"No, thank you." She was starting to look at me funny, and I figured it was time to leave.

"Well, thanks for the information."

She watched me as I went down the stairs, and then I heard her door close.

If the apartment underneath Ray's had been vacant for so long, who were the man and woman I'd seen on the bed? Had they broken in just to use it for sex, or were they there for another reason?

I went outside, back to the fire escape, and worked my way up to the fourth floor. I was getting familiar with the route.

On four I stopped and pressed my face to the window. There was a bed with a mattress, but no sheets or pillowcases. There didn't seem to be any other furniture. The mattress was cheap and thin, one of those pin-striped ones. There was nothing else in the room except for something under the bed. I pressed my face to the window again, cupped my hand around it, squinted, and made it out to be a Dunkin' Donuts bag.

15

I‌T WAS PRETTY clear to me now that somebody had been staking out Ray's apartment. Okay, maybe it wasn't so clear, but it was a good theory. Why should I think that I was the only one looking for him?

I was still puzzled, though, by the man and woman having been in bed together. Had they leaped in to bed when they'd heard me on the fire escape? Or had they been overcome by lust while on stakeout? And who were they? Cops? Bad guys? Knowing Ray, it could have been either, even without his involvement in the Pesce murder case.

There really wasn't much more I could do until I talked with Heck. I checked out a few places I knew Ray hung out—bars, a couple of gyms, a pool hall—but nobody had seen him for days. I finally gave up on Ray for a while and headed uptown to meet with Stan Waldrop's agent.

It was three-fifty-five when I stepped off the elevator on the eleventh floor and walked to the door marked JONATHAN HEALY ASSOCIATES. The office building was on Seventh Avenue in the fifties, just a couple of blocks west of the CBS building.

The woman walking to the chair behind the desk could have been an actress. I don't know if she had the ability, but she certainly had the looks. She was wearing a solid blue, silk, double-breasted jacket and matching skirt with a white lace top visible beneath it. The high heels she wore were the same shade of blue as the suit. Her stockings were flesh-toned nylons. Her hair was that shade that's too dark to be blond, but too light to be anything else. Her eyes were a startling blue, and she bore an amazing resemblance to that actress who had played on the final season of *Charlie's Angels* and had then gone on to play Sheena of the Jungle in a movie—Tanya Roberts.

"Can I help you?"

She had a deep voice, the one I'd heard on the phone earlier in the day.

"Yes, I'm here to see Mr. Healy."

"Do you have an appointment?"

"He's expecting me," I said. "My name is Jacoby."

"One moment." She used the intercom. "Mr. Jacoby is here, Mr. Healy."

"Send him in." The voice was tinny over the intercom, but I recognized it anyway.

"Go right in."

I hesitated.

"Has anyone ever told you you look like—"

"All the time." She rolled her eyes. "I wish she'd never made that jungle movie."

I nodded and went right in.

Healy turned out to be a tall, dark-haired man in his late fifties. He was seated behind his desk, wearing a white shirt and a green tie, which had been loosened. There was a jacket on the back of his char that was—I swear—purple. Judging from the stale smell in the office, and the overflowing ashtray, he was a heavy smoker. Even so, he did not have a cigarette lit at the moment.

"Jacoby?"

"That's right."

He didn't rise, but he did offer his hand for a very brief, unenthusiastic handshake.

"Sit, sit. You literally have . . ." he checked his watch ". . . twelve minutes."

"I'll do the best I can. Stan Waldrop came to me yesterday morning and hired me to find out who stole his jokes."

"How did they do that?"

"Apparently, right out of his computer."

As I said that he looked at his computer for a moment, and then back at me.

"What do you want from me?"

"Well, for one thing, you can tell me about Stan Waldrop."

"He's a comic with a mediocre talent."

"Then why do you represent him?"

"Because he works," Healy said. "When he stops bringing in money, I'll stop representing him."

"Do you see him hitting it big in the future?"

"No, but then who heard of Jerry Seinfeld a few years ago?"

"So you keep him on, just in case."

"As I said, Mr. Jacoby," he answered, looking at his watch, "he works."

"Does he usually worry about people stealing his jokes?"

"Actually," Healy said, "I don't see much of Stan. I have begun letting Miss Legend handle some of my . . . less important clients."

"Miss Legend?"

"The young woman sitting outside?"

"Oh," I said, "Miss Legend." How fitting. "What's Miss Legend's first name?"

"Andrea."

"May I speak to her about this?"

"Of course."

"Then I can probably finish up here a few minutes early," I said, standing up.

"I appreciate that."

"Oh, one thing."

"Yes."

"How long have you represented Stan?"

"About four years."

"Okay, Mr. Healy, you've been very helpful."

"Mmm," he said, and looked at his watch.

16

"MISS LEGEND."

She looked up from her desk, which was fairly clean. There was a laptop computer on it, though, and that's what she was looking at as I came out of Healy's office.

"Yes?"

"I understand from Mr. Healy that you handle Stan Waldrop's bookings."

"I do."

"Does that mean you spend much time talking with him?"

She sat back in her chair, which did nice things for her chest—which didn't need much help. I admit to loving to look at beautiful women, and I admit to having sexist thoughts when I do. I don't apologize for it. Like Elvis said in *Jailhouse Rock*, "it's the beast in me."

"We speak on the phone. I've had lunch with him a couple of times."

If it had been lunchtime, I would have asked her to have lunch with me.

I explained to her why I'd been hired by Waldrop, and then asked the same question I'd asked her boss, about Stan having his jokes stolen.

"He's mentioned it once or twice."

"Mentioned it how, exactly?"

"Just that he thought somebody might be trying to steal his act."

"Was he . . . insistent about it?"

She smiled.

"I think what you want to know is if he was paranoid about it."

Smart woman.

"That's it exactly."

"No, he wasn't. In fact, I don't think he worried about it any more than most entertainers."

"Miss Legend—may I call you Andrea?"

She hesitated, probably wondering if she'd ever see me again.

"I don't see why not, Mr. . . . ?"

"Jacoby."

Put me in my place. Nicely done.

"Andrea, how do you grade Stan as a comic?"

"He's . . . funny."

"Is that all?"

"Mr. Jacoby—"

"Miles."

She hesitated, probably wondering again.

"Miles . . . that is just about the highest praise you can give a comic."

"I see," I said. "Then you think he deserves the highest praise?"

"I think," she said slowly, "that he's funny."

And that seemed to be all I was going to get out of Andrea Legend.

"One more thing, if you don't mind?"

"Of course not."

"When I asked Stan who his agent was, he gave me Mr. Healy's name, not yours. Why is that?"

"The agency belongs to Mr. Healy, and it is the agency that represents the client."

"So technically speaking, you're not Stan's agent, Mr. Healy is."

"That's right."

"I see. Well, Miss Legend—Andrea—thanks for your help."

"May I ask a question?"

"Sure."

"Do you think somebody stole his jokes?"

"Well, there's a big blank space in his computer where they used to be."

"I hope you can help him then."

"I hope so too. Thanks."

I would have loved to call her Andy, but didn't dare. I wondered, as the elevator door closed, if anyone had that right.

▽

17

IT WAS FIVE-FIFTEEN when I got off the elevator on Heck's floor. When I walked in I didn't expect to find Missy there, but she was seated behind her desk.

"Hi."

"Hello, Miles."

"Working late?"

"I'm just waiting for Heck," she said, and then added hastily, "we're going to have dinner."

"Is he here?"

"Go right in. He's waiting for you."

"Thanks."

I went into Heck's office, where he was seated behind his desk in shirtsleeves, writing something.

"*Momento,*" he said, and I wondered if he was so deep in concentration that he hadn't realized he'd spoken Spanish to me.

I sat down and waited for him to finish what he was doing.

"I'm sorry," he said, finally looking up. "I was just making some notes."

"That's okay. How was your day?"

"My morning was very interesting, the rest of the day about the same as any other."

"Your interview?"

He nodded.

"What's Pesce have to say for himself?"

"He's charged with killing a bookie named Michael Bonetti. Know him?"

"I know of him."

"Is there a Bonetti Family that I should know about?"

"He's got a family, but not the way you mean."

He nodded his satisfaction with my answer.

"Bonetti was beaten to death."

"Is Pesce the type?"

"He's not a bruiser, but I guess he could have done it."

"Did he?"

"He says no."

"Who does he say did it?"

Heck hesitated, and I knew the answer before he said it. "Ray Carbone."

"No."

"He says he hired Carbone as a bodyguard, and it was in that capacity that Carbone killed Bonetti."

"What do the cops say about that?"

Heck shook his head. "Bonetti has not told this to the police."

"Why not?"

"He says Carbone saved his life, and he won't rat him out."

"He's going to be a stand-up guy on this and take the rap?"

"Not exactly. He wants us to find Carbone and get him to come in on his own. If it looks like we're going to go to trial without Carbone, then he'll talk."

"That won't get him off the hook."

"Maybe not, but it will have the cops looking for Ray as more than just a material witness."

"Do you believe him?"

"I don't have to believe him to defend him, Miles."

"Help me out here, Heck. Do you believe him?"

"I'm not sure. He seems sincere, but I've dealt with clients before who have seemed sincere and then confessed—also seeming sincere."

"But you're going to defend him?"

"Yes."

"What about Tyler?"

"What about him?"

"Will he be co-counsel?"

"No."

"Tyler was on Ray's answering machine tape, two messages, probably left before he came to see you."

Heck frowned. "So he tried to contact Ray before contact-
ing us. That wasn't what Pesce wanted."

"Maybe Tyler figured that if he could turn up Ray, Pesce
would let him handle the defense."

"Maybe," Heck said, still frowning. "I'll talk to him about
it. What else did you find out?"

"Nobody in Ray's building has seen him for a few days.
He's the super, so if he was there somebody would have seen
him. I still haven't talked to everyone, so I'll be going back.
I also talked to Joy, his girlfriend, and she hasn't seen him
since Monday night. When was the murder?"

"Saturday night."

"How did the cops get onto Pesce?"

"He looked good for it, and when they questioned him he
had bruised hands."

"What's he say about that?"

"He says he got in a fight with someone else."

"That what he told you?"

"Yes. He said he got in a fight with two of Bonetti's men,
which is why he called Ray for protection."

"I've got to tell you, Heck, I don't see it. Ray's a hard guy,
but he knows when to stop hitting somebody. He wouldn't
just beat somebody to death."

"Then find him for me."

"And if he says he didn't do it?"

"I'll have just as much reason to believe him as Pesce."

"Except for one thing."

"What's that?"

"Pesce's your client."

18

LINDA MATELLA HAD beauty-contest looks. There was no other way to put it. She was tall, about five ten, and blond—she was lots of blond! She was probably too full-bodied to have been a real beauty-contest winner. But along with the face, and hair, and body, and long, incredible legs, Linda had a brain. She had the makings of a good cop, maybe a good detective, but the last time I had seen her she was about to give it up. She said they just weren't giving her a chance because of her looks, and she was fed up with fielding all the remarks and innuendos.

"I'm tired of working as a dispatcher," she'd said, "and they won't transfer me to a precinct."

As I rode up the elevator of her building—which was on West End Avenue and Eighty-third Street—I was hoping things had changed for her. It would be a shame to see her waste the five years she had on the job.

Before going to pick Linda up I'd made the call I wanted to make to Saxon, in L.A. His assistant, a lady named Jo Zeidler, told me to hold on and then put me through.

I hadn't called him before, so we went through the amenities first.

"Eddie was a good man," he said finally. "I'm honored to be in his book. What can I do for you, Mr. Jacoby?"

"Miles."

"Okay, Miles. How can I help?"

"You're an actor as well as a PI, right?"

"Some people might argue that point, but yes, essentially you're right."

"I've got a case here involving somebody in show business. He's a stand-up comic."

"That's a funny coincidence. I just recently had a case involving a comedian."

"What kind of people am I dealing with, Saxon? As a whole, I mean."

"As a whole the comedian—or stand-up comic—might be the saddest person I know . . ."

He went on to explain that, like any performer, they were either not getting enough credit, or they were getting too much credit, and they didn't know how to do either gracefully.

"They've been dealing in laughs so long, though, that they're constantly reaching for one, even in the most serious situations."

"How much, uh, stealing goes on among them? I mean, stealing of jokes, uh, material."

"You've probably heard the old Henny Youngman stories?"

"Yes, I have. I, uh, thought they were old stories until I talked to my client."

"Henny Youngman had a brilliant delivery. He and the other older comics, like Berle and Benny, were always teasing about stolen jokes. These days comics' routines are so individual I would think less of it went on. After all, who could deliver lines the way Robin Williams does? He's a brilliant improv man."

"Improv."

"He improvises from moment to moment the way Jonathan Winters used to do. I'm sure he never writes anything down. Even if he did, it would change ten times before it finally came out of his mouth."

"But it does go on, right?"

He hesitated, then said, "I'm more at home talking about

actors and actresses, Miles. Maybe I should give you the phone number of a friend of mine."

"Who's that?"

"A comic named Tommy Sledge. Maybe you've seen him on cable. He does his act dressed as a classic PI."

"I have seen him." Just once, I remembered, while I was in a bar that had cable. They had HBO on, and this guy came out with the trench coat, fedora, cigarette, and a rapid-fire delivery of funny lines. He started on stage and then worked the audience brilliantly, getting them involved in the act, all the time staying in the persona of a hardboiled PI. I remembered thinking that he was the perfect cliché. Me, I don't even own a trench coat.

"Maybe Tommy can help you out."

He gave me Sledge's number, and I wrote it in my notebook.

"Give him a call," Saxon said. "Hopefully, he's in town and not on tour. He's a busy guy."

"I'll give him a try. Thanks, Saxon. I owe you."

"I'll collect."

I tried Tommy Sledge immediately, but got no answer. I decided to try him again tomorrow. It was time to pick up Linda and catch Stan Waldrop's act.

Linda gave me a long hug. She felt good and looked good, and I told her so. She was wearing a white lace bodysuit under a chocolate-colored blazer, with off-white trousers. She was the second woman I had seen that day wearing a lace top of some kind. I'm dense, but I'd guess they were in style.

"Jesus, you smell great too," I said, releasing her reluctantly.

"New perfume." She stepped back into the apartment to let me enter.

"What's it called?"

" 'Red'."

I didn't say, "Couldn't you find one called 'Blond'?" She got enough of that kind of thing at work.

"Are you ready to go? I've got a cab downstairs."

"I just need a minute."

She took ten, but it was worth the wait. In heels she was just a little taller than I was, but that didn't bother me. I just stood next to her in the elevator and felt good.

"Where are we going again?"

"I have an address in the Village, on Bleecker, but he didn't give me the name of the place."

"Who didn't?"

"Oh, I'm sorry. His name's Stan Waldrop, he's a stand-up comic."

"I never heard of him."

"Good."

"Why?"

"I want your honest opinion of him."

"Is it important?"

"Not really. I just want to know if you think he's funny."

In the cab she asked, "Is this business or pleasure?"

"He's a new client."

"What's his problem?"

It took the rest of the ride for me to explain it to her. When we reached our destination, I saw that the place was new, but the location was old. I knew of at least four other clubs or restaurants that had tried to make a go of it here in the last year and a half and had failed. This time it was called "The Comic Look." Obviously, it was a straight comedy club.

We went inside, and I stopped at the box office to give my name.

"Sure, Jacoby," the guy in the cage said, pronouncing it the way it looked instead of the proper way, "Jack-o-bee." I let it ride.

He handed me two tickets while staring past me at Linda. I let that ride too. If I was going to get upset at every man who stared at her, I'd be mad at the world.

"This is your guy, huh?" Linda asked, pointing to a poster on the wall.

It was a bad likeness of Waldrop, but it actually made him better looking than he really was.

"That's him."

"What's his gimmick?"

"I've never caught his act. This will be my first time too."

She stared at me and said, "Why does everything some men say sound dirty?"

I said "Wha—" helplessly, feigning outrage, and we went inside.

$\triangledown$

19

THE FLOOR WAS crowded with small tables, with very little
space between them. Apparently, the tickets I had were good
ones because the guy I gave them to showed us to a table
down in the front. The stage was a riser with a stool on it,
and a brick-wall backing with the words, in neon, THE
COMIC LOOK. There was a microphone sitting on the stool
at the moment.

"I'm impressed," Linda said as we sat.

"Didn't know I had such influence, huh?" I leaned toward
her and asked, "Is it true women find this kind of thing
sexy?"

She leaned toward me, giving me a good whiff of her "Red,"
which was rapidly becoming my favorite perfume.

"Influence is impressive," she said in a low voice, "but
power is sexy. Keep working."

I laughed, and as I sat back I looked past her and saw
Andrea Legend being shown to an even better table than
ours. She had changed her clothes. Now she was wearing a
sleeveless black jacket and a pair of wide, billowy, black-and-
white print pants.

Linda noticed my look and turned around to take a
look-see herself.

"She's beautiful. Do you know her?"

"She's Stan's agent. Her name's Andrea Legend."

"Really? That's really her last name?"

"Yes, really."

"And who's the man?"

I didn't know who the man was. He was young, maybe late twenties, and very good-looking. His hair was longish, and he had an earring in each ear à la George Michael, with the same kind of beard stubble. He was wearing a black silk sports jacket with a green T-shirt underneath.

"He's adorable," Linda said.

"You think so?"

She looked at me and said, teasingly, "Oh yes, very sexy."

"Glad to hear it."

"Why don't you go and say hello?"

"I think I will. Want to come?"

"No, I'll stay here," she said. "I might suffer by comparison."

"Never happen."

I walked over and started to wonder how I'd fare by comparison, but decided to forget it.

Andrea Legend saw me coming and said something to the man that made him look too.

"Hello, Miss Legend."

She smiled and said, "I thought we decided to use first names . . . Miles?"

"Andrea," I said. "I didn't know you'd be here, or I would have said something earlier about coming together."

"As you can see," she said, indicating the man next to her, "I made do—as I see you have. She's lovely."

"Thank you."

"This is Bill Allegretto. Bill is another of my—our—clients."

I shook hands with Bill, but as I tried to release it he held on. He wasn't trying to match grips, he just wasn't ready to let go, yet.

"Andy tells me you're a private detective."

"Yes . . . and you?"

"Oh, I'm a comedian."

He finally let go of my hand.

"Bill is very up-and-coming, and has great things ahead of him."

"I'm really an actor, but I seem to have a flare for comedy."

"Really?"

"It's comedy with an edge," Andrea hastened to add, "a sexy edge."

"Really." I was still working on his calling her "Andy." I was trying to read their body language, but while they were sitting close, they weren't touching.

"Think you can learn something by watching Stan?" I asked.

Bill laughed at that and gave Andrea a "where-did-you-get-this-guy" look.

"Well," I said, "maybe not."

"Enjoy the show, Miles . . . and call me. I'd like to know what you think."

"Okay," I said. "I'll call."

Bill and I shook hands again and I waited until I was back at my table to wipe mine on my jeans.

"Who is he?" Linda asked, turning to look again. Somehow Andy and Bill were already being served drinks, and Bill raised his to Linda, who smiled back.

"Hey," I said, "I'm over here."

"Are they . . . together?" she asked.

"Why? You want to hit on him?"

She smiled an impossibly beautiful and wide smile, showing lots of pretty white teeth. I thought Linda Matella was probably the most beautiful woman I'd ever been within ten feet of. I wondered why I hadn't tried to get her in bed, yet. Was I thinking that because I was jealous?

"Miles . . ." She packed a lot into my name.

"Okay, okay, I'm sorry. His name is Bill Allegretto and he's another of Andrea's clients."

"A comic?"

I nodded.

"Apparently, with an edge . . . a sexy edge."

"I can believe it," she said, but she had the good grace not to turn around for another look.

"Where's the waitress?" I groused. "I want a beer."

▽

20

WHEN I HAD a beer and Linda had a screwdriver, we started to catch up a bit as the place filled. I finally asked her how things were going with her job.

"I've had it, Miles. I'm handing in my papers and getting out."

"Gee, Linda, I'm sorry to hear that. What are you going to do?"

"I don't know yet. I've got some money saved, but in a few months I'm going to need a job pretty badly. I could go back to school, but I'm twenty-eight."

"Way over the hill."

"I know people have gone back even later, but I hated school. I was good at it, but I hated it. I thought I'd found what I wanted in police work. God, I loved the academy. It wasn't like school at all. When they first assigned me to police headquarters I said okay, for a while, but now I know they'll never let me out."

"Do you have anything in mind?"

"Well," she said, "I could be a PI—don't worry, I'm not asking you for a job. I was been thinking about some kind of security work. You know, like for those private agencies that patrol neighborhoods?"

It wasn't such an outrageous idea, considering I was going to be partnered with Walker.

I told her about that, because after all we *were* catching up.

"Oh, Miles, if you need a woman for anything—"

"I know, Linda. I've already thought of that."

"Oh, God," she said, covering her mouth with her hand, "I *am* asking for a job."

"Why don't we just see what happens? I can't promise you anything, but something might come up for you. Meanwhile, keep your options open."

I checked my watch and saw that Stan was ten minutes late getting on stage. I glanced around. The club seemed pretty full, with just a few empty seats in the back. Other people were looking at their watches also, like Andrea Legend. She was frowning, leaning over and saying something to Allegretto. As a couple they were drawing a lot of admiring glances. I looked and figured that she and Linda were the best-looking women in the place. Maybe I was keeping Linda from getting the attention she deserved.

"Where is he?" Linda asked. "Wasn't he supposed to be on by now?"

"Yeah, he was."

"Maybe he doesn't remember any of his jokes."

I looked at her.

"Well, from what you told me in the car . . ."

"I know, it's a possibility."

I looked at Andrea just as a man hurried over to her, leaned down, and said something in her ear with some urgency. From the look on her face it was shocking news. She surprised me then by getting up and walking toward us.

"Miles," she said, ignoring Linda and grabbing my arm tightly, "I need your help."

"What is it?"

"Can you come backstage?"

"Why?"

"Something's wrong."

I looked at Linda and said, "Come on."

"Oh, I meant, just you . . ."

"This is Linda Matella, Andrea," I said, "she's a police officer."

"Oh!" Andrea gave Linda a funny look. "Well, I guess you had better come too, then."

Linda stood up and we followed Andrea backstage. I noticed that Bill Allegretto was staying right where he was.

When we got backstage, the man who had spoken to Andrea was waiting.

"Who is she?" he asked, pointing to Linda.

In response Linda took out her shield and ID card and hung it from the pocket of her blazer.

"Oh," the man said.

"Who are you?" Linda asked, taking charge.

"Harry Joel . . . uh, I'm the manager."

"What's the problem?"

"Uh, in Stan's dressing room."

"Show us."

Joel, Andrea, Linda, and I walked along a hall to Stan's dressing room. The door was closed. When Linda opened it, we all saw Stan lying on the floor, on his back.

"Is he dead?" I asked.

"I don't know," Joel said. "I sent one of my assistants back here to see that was taking him so long, and she found him. The poor kid's in hysterics."

"Miles . . ." Linda said.

She had never been faced with a body before.

"Let's take a look at him," I said to her, my stomach feeling hollow. This was the last thing I expected. Maybe he'd just fainted, or he was sick . . . something. As we stepped into the room, I hoped for something other than what it appeared to be.

I leaned over him and checked. His body was warm, but there was no pulse at all.

"Damn it." I shook my head.

Linda turned and pointed at the manager.

"Do you have security?"

"Uh, yeah . . . I mean, I got bouncers—"

"Nobody in or out until the police arrive. Understand?"

"Uh, sure, but—?"

"Who else knows about this?"

"Just us, and Sherry—that's the girl I sent back here."

"Where is she?"

"In my office."

"Make sure she doesn't tell anyone what she found. I need a phone."

"There's a pay phone out here."

"Miles," she said, "I'll call it in."

"I'll stay here," I said, staring down at my dead client.

Shit, I hadn't even gotten the chance to work on his case, I was so wrapped up in finding Ray Carbone . . . and now this.

Fuck!

▽

21

I KEPT HARRY Joel and Andrea Legend with me, even though she wanted to leave.

"What happened to him?"

I leaned over again and examined Stan Waldrop without touching him. There was blood underneath his head. I hadn't seen it the first time because it only showed on the left side of his head, the side away from me. The floor must have slanted that way.

"It looks like he was hit on the head from behind." I stood up and looked at Andrea. "When was the last time you saw him?"

"I haven't seen him in over a week."

"Not tonight?"

"No," she said, "when I got here I went right to my table."

"When did you talk to him last?"

"That was today."

"When?"

"After I talked to you, I called him to see if he was all right for tonight. I also told him he should have called us before hiring you."

"What did he say?"

"We agreed that we'd talk about that tonight, after his performance."

I looked down at Stan. No more talking, no more jokes, no more worries—for him, anyway.

Linda returned and said to me, "They're rolling from the Sixth."

"We'll all wait here."

At that moment a man came rushing up to Joel and said, "Harry, they're gonna tear the house down—" He stopped short when he saw Stan's body. "Jesus."

"Talk to him," I said to Joel. "Make sure he doesn't say anything to anyone."

Joel pushed the man out of the doorway, then came back in himself.

"I've got to do something. People are starting to get restless, and a few want to leave already."

"Don't you have anyone else you can put on?"

"No, Stan was it."

"Bill."

I looked at Andrea.

"Bill Allegretto. He can go on."

"Is he a comic?" Joel asked.

"Yes."

"Can I?" Joel asked. He wasn't sure whether he should talk to me or Linda, so he looked at us both.

Linda looked at me.

"I don't see why not. Get him back here, though. Andrea, you tell him he has to go on because Stan's sick."

"Why not tell him the truth?"

"It might shake him up, and then he won't be able to go on. As it stands now, we need him to keep everyone occupied until the police arrive." I looked at Joel and said, "Get him."

As Joel left I looked at Andrea and said, "Don't tell him about this, okay?"

"All right," she said, probably feeling a little stressed out. "I have to call my boss."

"No, not until the cops are done."

"You said she was a cop."

"We need the detectives here to take charge," I said. "Once they're here, you can argue with them. For now just go along with us."

"All right, all right."

"Let's go outside," I suggested. "We should close this door."

Out in the hall, Joel arrived with a puzzled looking Allegretto. Andrea talked to him for a few minutes and he nodded.

"The show must go on," Linda said under her breath.

$\triangledown$

22

WHEN THE DETECTIVES from the Sixth Precinct arrived, they took over. Linda identified herself and I could see immediately what she had been going through in the department. The two detectives who responded were Mark Pell and Christopher Matthews. Pell seemed to be the lead man, and a little young to be a detective. Matthews was older, and he immediately began calling Linda "sweetheart" and looking her up and down.

She pushed through it, explaining both her presence and mine, although I was almost immediately evicted from the crime scene and exiled outside with the rest of the crowd.

The audience had been laughing at whatever Allegretto was doing onstage when the police arrived. While they were looking over the body and the scene, Allegretto finished onstage. That was when the people tried to leave and found out they couldn't. They grumbled, but it was finally explained to them that a murder had occurred on the premises, the police were on the scene, and no one was going to be permitted to leave without being questioned.

I was the first questioned because I knew the victim. Actually, I was probably the first after Andrea Legend.

Thankfully, when Linda came out to find me it was with Detective Mark Pell.

Pell appeared to be in his twenties, though I doubted it. I figured he was just young-looking, and was more likely in his early thirties. He was a tall, slender man with large framed glasses and a face that hardly looked touched by a razor yet. I was willing to bet he knew a little bit about what Linda had gone through the last five years. Even though he had risen to the level of detective, he must have taken countless ribbings along the way for his appearance.

"Mr. Jacoby?"

"That's right."

"I have a few questions."

"I'm all yours."

He paused and looked at Linda.

"I'd like to speak to Mr. Jacoby alone, Officer?"

Linda looked at me, then said, "Oh, sure, Detective."

Pell took me into the manager's office, which had been "donated" by Harry Joel for the purpose of interviews. I sat in a chair and Pell perched a hip on the desk. The walls were covered with photos of comics who certainly hadn't appeared here, since the place was fairly new. Maybe they were the Harry Joel private collection, and maybe the photos came with the frames.

"Officer Matella tells me you knew the victim."

"Yes, he was a client."

"May I see your ID, please?"

He was real polite, and I decided to try and get through this as painlessly as possible, holding little back and not cracking wise. I took out the photostat of my license and handed it to him. He looked at it briefly, nodded, and handed it back.

"The victim hired you?"

"Yes."

"To do what?"

"He thought someone had gotten into his computer and stolen his jokes."

"His jokes?"

"Yes."

"He wrote them all down?"

"I guess so."

"Did he know who did it?"

"No, that's why he hired me."

Oops. Did that qualify as a wisecrack?

"Look," Pell said, "some of my questions may sound stupid. How about you just answer them without comment?"

"I'll try."

"He wrote all his jokes down on computer?"

"Yes."

"Hard disk or floppy?"

"What?" He might as well have spoken Greek to me.

"Never mind. I'll ask his agent. When was the last time you saw . . ."

The rest of the questions were standard. When and where had I last seen him? Talked to him? My impressions of him. Had he given me any names of people he suspected? Was he nervous? Blah, blah, blah . . .

When he was done, he closed his notebook and placed it in his inside jacket pocket.

"We're finished with you, Mr. Jacoby. You can go."

I was grateful for that. I knew they were going to be there a long time questioning people.

"What about Linda?"

"Who?"

"Officer Matella. Will she be staying to help out?"

Pell frowned.

"No," he said, as if I were crazy. "You can take her home."

"She did a good job here, Detective. That should be reflected in your report."

"I write my own reports, Mr. Jacoby, thank you."

"I just wanted you to know."

"I'll send her out to you."

He pushed off the desk and started for the door.

"What about Miss Legend?"

He turned and said, "I've questioned her. She's free to go too." He gave me a long look and then asked, "You want her too?"

I decided to regard the question as innocent, and not fraught with hidden meaning.

"No," I said, "just Officer Matella will do, thanks."

$\triangledown$

23

THE FIRST PERSON I told about Stan Waldrop's murder was Geneva.

"Second day in a row before opening," she said as I walked in. She was wearing another variation of what she usually wore, something loose on the outside with something athletic underneath. The colors were vivid today—cranberry and yellow?—and over her left breast was the word MUSCLE.

"Maybe I can start coming in late."

When I didn't banter back she stopped what she was doing and walked over to me.

"What happened?"

"I lost a client last night."

"You get fired?"

"No, he got killed."

She stared at me for a few moments, then said, "I'll get some coffee. You sit down."

I sat in a booth and she returned with two cups.

"Give."

I told her what had happened last night.

"Is that in the papers today?" she asked.

"I don't know, I haven't even looked, yet."

I stared across the table at Geneva.

"Lucky for you there was a cop with you last night, huh?" she said.

"Yeah, lucky."

Linda didn't think it was so lucky. After we left the club, she had been very quiet in the cab. Actually, she didn't speak

at all until we got to her door. After she put her key in the
lock, she turned to me and put her hand on my chest.

"I need to . . . digest what happened tonight."

"I know. It was a shock."

"That's putting it mildly."

"I'm sorry it turned out . . . the way it did."

"I'm sorry for you, and your client, but I think this is going
to help me make my final decision."

"You were great tonight, Linda."

She smiled and kissed my cheek. "I'll call you, okay?"

"Okay." I rode down in the elevator wondering if I'd ever
hear from her again.

"I really know how to show a lady a good time," I said to
Geneva.

"How was you to know what was gonna happen?"

"The detectives who responded treated her shabbily, Gen.
This could have been a big break for her. She was a little
shaky in spots, but she handled herself real well."

"Welcome to the real world," she said. "I go through that
at the gym. Sure there's men there and I want them to notice
me, but they always seem to notice me for the wrong reason."
She looked down at her chest and added, "Or reasons."

I caught myself staring again, and looked away.

"What are you gonna do now?"

"Well, I thought I'd go in and talk to the detectives today,
see what they've got."

"You gonna work on this murder? I thought you told me
that PIs don't work on open homicides."

"You really listen to me when I talk to you?"

She made a face and said, "Just about unimportant stuff."

"I don't think I'm going to work on it," I said. "I just want
to see what they've got."

"What about what he asked you to do for him?"

I shook my head. "What good would it do now to find out
who stole his jokes?"

"He pay you?"

"For a few days."

"You gonna give the money back?"

"To whom? I don't know if he had any family."

"You ain't gonna give the money back, but you been paid to do a job."

"You going to lecture me on morals now?"

"Nope," she said, sliding out of the booth and picking up both empty coffee cups from the table. "I ain't lecturing today. I was just talkin'."

▽

24

I WENT INTO my office with another cup of coffee and sat at my desk. What were the morals involved? When Aaron Steinway hired me to find his collection of pulp magazines, and then was killed, I worked until his killer was caught. After that I stopped looking for the magazines. My reasoning was that I wasn't being paid anymore.

By applying the same reasoning here, I still owed Stan Waldrop a couple of days of looking for his stolen jokes. I figured that was what I'd do. That wasn't even factoring in the guilt I felt for not having done any work on his case at the time of his murder.

Of course, I couldn't let that guilt, in turn, keep me from working on what I'd come to think of as Ray's case. As far as Heck was concerned, this was Danny Pesce's case. I had a little different slant on it.

I picked up my phone, dialed Ray's number, waited for the beep, and then keyed in his code number. There was only one message.

"Ray? Are you there? Ray?" Click.

The voice was Joy's, and she sounded worried. At least I knew that she wasn't lying to me. She really didn't know where he was, or why would she be calling his number and leaving a message?

I looked at my own machine for the first time that morning. The red light was steady, and that suited me. I hated messages, but I also hated missing important calls when I was working.

I sat back in my chair and went over the events of the night before, including my interview with Detective Pell. He'd said something I didn't understand, and I wanted it clarified. For that I needed somebody who knew computers. The closest person to me for that was Marty.

I went back outside to find Geneva behind the bar, still setting up for the day.

"Gen, is Marty working today?"

"Yep. He's comin' in at four. Ed should be in any minute."

"You don't have a computer, do you?"

She looked at me and said, "That little recorder I gave you yesterday is the most sophisticated piece of equipment I own. Sorry."

It always amazed me how easily Gen went from her street talk to a more polished speech pattern.

I went back into my office and called the Sixth Precinct. Even though I thought I knew the answer I just wanted to make sure. When the phone was answered, I asked for the squad, and when the call was put through I asked for Detective Pell's hours.

"He's workin' a four to twelve today," a man's voice said. "Can I help you? I'm Detective Parnell."

"No, thanks," I said, "I'll call back later."

I couldn't talk to Pell or Marty until after four. I picked up the phone again and dialed John Healy's office. I was pretty sure he'd be out to lunch, but maybe . . ."

"Jonathan Healy."

"Andrea, it's Miles Jacoby."

There was a very distinct hesitation, and then, "Oh . . . hello."

"How are you?"

"Trying to recover, I'm afraid. It was . . . such a shock."

"You must have mixed feelings about last night."

"I don't understand."

"Well, you lost one client, but the other did fairly well, didn't he?"

"If you mean Bill Allegretto, he hardly needed that kind

of exposure." She sounded very defensive, leading me back
to the thoughts I was having the night before about the exact
nature of their relationship. "He performed as a favor to me."

"I see. Too much of a big fish for that small club?"

"Exactly."

"Unlike Stan."

"Stan was a stand-up, and that's all. Bill is an actor."

Touchy.

"Why did you call?"

"I was wondering if you had a key to Stan Waldrop's
apartment?"

Another pause.

"Why?"

"I'd like to get inside. I still have a job to do."

"But no one's paying you—"

"Stan paid me for a few days in advance. I figure I owe it
to him to play out the string."

"I see . . . well, no, I don't have a key. Why would I?"

"Well, I'm not suggesting that anything was going on
between you two," I said, "I just thought he might have left
an extra key to his place with his agent, that's all."

"Well . . . no, he didn't."

"All right, then. I don't suppose we'll, uh, have any reason
to see each other after this."

"Well . . . if you find those jokes, I suppose you should
turn them over to us."

"To you?"

"What else would you do with them?"

"I really hadn't thought about it. Family?"

"He didn't have any."

"Well then, I suppose turning them over to you would
make sense. In that case, I hope to see you again, soon."

"Yes," she said, without much enthusiasm, "soon."

▽

25

W<small>HEN</small> I <small>WENT</small> back out to the bar, Steve Stilwell was sitting there talking to Geneva.

"There he is," he said as I appeared.

"Hello, Steve. How are things with you?"

"Not as bad as they are with you. I hear you lost one last night."

"Where did you hear that?"

He pointed to Geneva, who looked away.

"No, it's okay," I said, "I just wanted to see if you'd heard something from the job."

"I'm on suspension, remember?"

"I remember, I just thought you might be in contact with someone."

Stilwell and Taylor worked out of the Sixth Precinct building, although technically they were not assigned there.

"What did you have in mind?"

"Do you know a detective named Pell?"

"Mark? Sure."

"What do you think of him?"

"He's young, but he's on the rise. There's only one thing that might hurt him."

"What?"

"The same thing that hurt Serpico. He's just too damned clean."

"What about his partner?"

Stilwell frowned. "Who's he partnered with these days? They keep moving him around."

"Matthews."

"Chris Matthews," Stilwell said with a nod. "He won't last long with Pell, either."

"Why not?"

"He's a burnout. He'll be like a weight around Pell's neck."

"What's Pell's story? Does he have a rabbi?"

"That's the other thing that's gonna hurt him," Stilwell said. "He doesn't believe in them."

People in the department who wanted to go anywhere usually did it with a rabbi, some high-ranking official who could clear the way for them.

"Well, I'm really not interested in his career. Is he going to give me a hard time if I want to sniff around this case?"

"Oh, hell, yes. You try stickin' your nose in an active case and he'll be on you like white on rice."

"Where'd you hear that one?" Geneva asked, raising an eyebrow at him.

"I think I heard Hawk say it to Spenser once."

"Who?" I asked.

"You wouldn't know them," Geneva said. "They're characters in a book."

"And I don't read books?"

She put her hands on her hips and asked, "Well, do you?"

I frowned and said in a surly tone, "Once in a while."

"What's the last book you read?" The question was a challenge.

"I don't remember . . . something about Mike Tyson."

"See?" Geneva looked at Stilwell. "Sports book. We're talking mystery novels."

Stilwell stared at Geneva and said, "Hawk and Spenser are from books?"

"Where did you think they were from?"

"TV."

"Can I get in here with important stuff?" I asked.

Geneva turned away, muttering, "TV . . ."

"I'm going to see Pell later this afternoon."

"If you want to nose around in this case, don't tell him."

"Thanks for the advice. What have you and Bruce been up to?"

"We're nosing around our case. In fact, he's supposed to meet me here so we can compare notes on some things."

Something occurred to me at that moment.

"Steve?"

"Yeah?"

"Do you know Ray Carbone?"

"Sure, why?"

"Have you seen him lately?"

"Let me think . . . no, I don't think I've seen Ray in weeks, but then we don't hang out. I thought you guys did."

"Sometimes, but I haven't seen him for some time, either. In fact, nobody's seen him for days."

"Is he in trouble?"

"I think so. You know a guy named Danny Pesce?"

"Danny the Fish," Stilwell said. "He just got locked up for murder. Is Ray involved in that?"

"What do you know about Danny?"

"He rubs people the wrong way—like Mike Bonetti, the guy he's supposed to have killed."

"What do you know about Bonetti?"

"He was tough, Jack. Frankly, I don't see how somebody like the Fish could have . . . uh-oh."

I didn't say anything. In fact, I had the feeling I had gone too far.

"Is he sayin' Ray did it? Is that why you can't find him?".

"Steve, I can't answer that."

"You have no client confidentiality—wait a minute."

He was getting the hang of this piece by piece.

"Are you workin' for his attorney?"

"That's right."

"Tyler? That scumbag?"

"Heck Delgado is defending Danny Pesce."

Stilwell's eyes widened.

"Where does the Fish come off hiring Heck?"

"I guess he wanted the best."

"The best costs, Jack."

"Maybe he has a savings account. I don't know."

Stilwell gave me a long look and then said, "You know what? I'm gonna stop asking questions."

"Good."

"But I'm gonna offer you my help, if you need it."

"You know," I said, "there is something you can find out for me."

"What?"

I explained about the man and woman I had seen in the apartment below Ray's.

"You want me to find out if they were cops stakin' out his place?"

"Right."

"And if they weren't?"

"Then there's somebody else out there looking for Ray," I said, "and he may be on the run for his life."

▽

26

I PUTZED AROUND at the bar for a while, paying bills—the ones I could afford to pay—putting in orders for booze and food. A couple of times I tried Ray's number, but there were no new messages. I tried Joy once, but there was no answer there, either.

At two o'clock I decided to go over to The Comic Look and snoop around. When I got there, the front door was closed, but banging on it a few times with the heel of my hand solved that problem. The door was opened by Harry Joel, who frowned when he saw me.

"Miles Jacoby," I said before he could open his mouth. "I was here last night?"

"Oh, yeah," he said. "Whataya want?"

"I want in," I said. "I'd like to take a look around."

"The cops did that last night."

"That's right, they did. I didn't."

He frowned again. "You ain't a cop."

"That's right," I said, trying to think of a good lie. "I'm a private detective. Stan's agent is concerned about your security."

"What?"

"Yeah," I said, warming to my subject, "I think he's wondering if he should risk any more of his talent here if you've got bad security."

"Our security had nothin' to do with what happened last night."

"Convince me."

He hesitated a moment, then swung the heavy metal door open and said, "Come on in."

He locked the door behind us, then turned to face me.

"Whataya wanna see?"

"Stan's dressing room first."

"This way."

I followed him through the darkened club and backstage, then down the same hall as the night before until we reached the room Stan Waldrop had died in. The blood that had been beneath his head had already been cleaned away. Whoever wielded the mop had done a damn good job.

"No other door in or out of this room?" I asked, looking around.

"No."

"Who's allowed backstage?"

"Nobody."

"You?"

"Yes."

"Your employees?"

"Yes."

"The performers."

"Yeah."

"And their employees . . ."

"Uh-huh."

". . . friends . . ."

"Uh, yeah . . ."

". . . and families."

"Um," he said, looking down.

"That's a helluva lot of 'nobody's'."

"Yeah," he said glumly.

I looked around the room some more. It was unimpressive, pretty cramped, with one makeup table for the performers who wanted to use makeup, or just make use of the mirror.

"Are there other dressing rooms?"

"Yeah, two others."

"Can I see those?"

"Why?"

"I'd just like to see as much as I can."

He shrugged and said, "Come on."

He showed me the other rooms, which were down the hall, one on the same side as Stan's and the other across the way. They were almost identical to Stan's.

"Is there a back door?"

"Yeah."

It was like pulling teeth.

"Show me."

He led me to the very end of the hall; a quick right and we were standing at another metal door. I tried it and found it locked.

"Is it always locked?"

"Always."

"Is this 'always' the same as your 'nobody'?"

"Huh?"

"Who has keys?"

"I do."

"Anyone else?"

"No."

"So there was no way for someone to kill Waldrop and then get out this way?"

"Not without my keys."

As soon as he said it, his eyes went wide.

"Hey, wait a minute—"

"Relax," I said, "I'm not looking to pin this on you. What's outside this door?"

"The alley, some garbage pails, that's it."

"Show me."

"The keys are in my desk."

I stared at him.

"You always keep the keys in your desk instead of on you?"

"No, not always."

"But enough so that somebody might have been able to make a copy?"

"Who would make a copy?"

I glared at him this time and said, "Somebody who wanted to kill Stan Waldrop and then get out this door."

"Shit," he said under his breath, coming down very hard on the "t."

"Any security back here during the show?"

"No, the security is out front to keep anyone from getting back here."

"Well, that's something. That means that no strangers could have gotten back here before the show last night?"

"That's right. We don't want the performers havin' to deal with fans before they go on."

"Twenty bucks in a security man's hand might make the difference, though, huh?"

"It would cost him his job."

And a high-paying, fringe-benefit cram-packed job it was too, I was sure.

"Okay," I said, "I've seen enough."

As he led me to the front door he asked, "What are you gonna tell Healy?"

"I'll tell him I made some suggestions to you. If you take them, then he might continue to place his talent here."

"What suggestions?"

"Keep your keys on you at all times, hire reliable security men, keep one out front and one in the hall outside the dressing rooms. That should do it."

"That's gonna cost me."

Just before I stepped out the door back into the light I said, "It'll cost you more if you don't do it."

▽

27

A̶T THREE-THIRTY I left Packy's and walked to the Sixth Precinct. I presented myself at the desk and said I wanted to see Detective Pell.

"Hang on," the desk sergeant said. He dialed the phone, spoke a few words, then leaned over and asked, "Who are you?"

"Jacoby."

"Says his name's Jacoby," I heard him relay. "Okay."

He hung up and asked, "You know where it is?"

"I know."

"Go ahead up."

"Thanks."

I took the stairs to the second floor and the squad room. I'd been there once or twice in the past, but not enough to recognize the faces I saw at the desks, or for them to recognize me.

"Mr. Jacoby," Pell said from his desk. "What can I do for you?"

"I just wanted to check in with you, see what you found out last night."

He was sitting behind his desk in a short-sleeved shirt. He wasn't muscular, but I could see that his arms were hard. He worked out.

"Why? Are you working for someone?"

"No," I said, and then added, "at least not on an active murder case."

"Ah, then what's your interest?"

"I think it will tie in with something else I'm working on."

"And who is your client?"

"Stan Waldrop."

He stared at me a moment. "The dead man?"

"That's right."

"Let me get this straight . . . you're working for a dead man?"

"Let me explain," I said. "Waldrop hired me two days ago to find out who was stealing his material. He paid me for several days in advance. I still feel a responsibility to him to try."

Considering how clean Stilwell said Pell was, I thought this was an argument that the young man would appreciate.

"Responsibility to a dead man?"

"Sounds dumb when you say it like that," I said, "but yeah."

He studied me for a few moments, probably trying to figure out if I was putting him on. I looked around and saw his partner slouched at the next desk, listening. The look on his face said that he knew I was slinging enough shit to bury us all. I figured the truth was somewhere between what he thought and what Pell was thinking.

"No, not dumb," he said finally. "I guess it's admirable . . . in a way."

"Look," I said, "if I keep looking for the stolen material maybe I'll come up with something I can pass on to you."

"And vice versa?"

"If you've a mind to, yeah."

"What's this material look like?"

"It was in a computer."

"Hard disk? Floppy?" I didn't know any more about that than I had last night.

"I don't really know what those words mean, Pell."

"If it was in his hard disk somebody could have accessed his computer by modem, but to do that they would have had to know the file name—unless, of course, he filed it as 'jokes', or something like that."

"What do you say, Detective?" I asked. "An exchange of information?"

"Don't do it," Matthews called out.

Pell looked at him.

"He's playin' you, junior."

"I've asked you not to call me that."

"Yeah, well, whatever, this dick is probably playin' on the fact that you're inexperienced. You're lucky I'm here to stop you from makin' a big mistake."

"It's my case, Matthews, and I'll conduct it as I see fit." Pell turned his eyes from his partner and looked at me. "If you're playing me for a sucker, Jacoby, you'll be sorry."

I probably would have taken that threat a little more seriously if he hadn't had such a baby face.

"You'll get everything I get, Detective."

"I can't make you the same promise, but I will try to give you anything I think will be helpful."

I frowned to show I didn't like it much.

"I guess that's as good as I'm going to get, huh?"

"That's it."

"Okay," I said, turning to leave, "I just didn't want you thinking I was getting in your way."

"You get in my way, dick," Matthews said, "and I'll roll right over you."

I probably would have taken *that* threat a little more seriously if he hadn't been such an obvious burnout.

"I'll remember that . . . Detective."

I looked at Pell, took out a business card, and handed it to him.

"I don't remember if you took my number last night."

He took my card, glanced at it, and then put it down on his desk very carefully.

"Just remember what I said."

I wanted to tell him that I thought we were all done with threats, but I decided to get out of there with our new state of cooperation intact instead of saying something that would shatter it before we even got started.

▽

28

From a pay phone I called Joy's number again and there
was no answer. If she wasn't home at this time of the
evening, I thought maybe she'd be at the small storefront
health club on Eighth Street in the West Village. I grabbed
a cab and had him drop me at Eighth Street and Sixth
Avenue, right in front of the big B. Dalton bookstore. The
health club she worked at was just down the street from
where the Eighth Street Cinema used to be.

The place had a front that was almost all glass, with some
vertical blinds on the inside. The blinds were tilted so that
no one looking in could see the leotard-clad women doing
their step aerobics.

I walked in and my nostrils were immediately assailed by
the scent of women exerting themselves. Don't ever let
anyone tell you that women don't sweat. It was as pungent
in that place as any men's locker room I'd ever been in during
my boxing days. Also, the airwaves were being pummeled by
Donna Summers's "She Works Hard for the Money" with
the bass on high.

At the moment there were about eighteen women standing in three rows of six being put through their paces by a
dark-haired girl in a purple leotard. The women ran the
gamut from skinny to plump, but none were grossly out of
shape. Maybe it was an advanced class.

I stood there watching for a few minutes, and the instructor
finally looked over at me. Her face was nowhere near a match
for her shape. Her nose was too long and sharp, her eyes too

close together, and she was older than she appeared when I couldn't see her face. There was some loose skin around her throat that apparently even aerobics couldn't help.

"Keep working, girls," she called out, and came over to see what I wanted. "Can I help you?"

The sharp smell of sweat in the air deepened as she stood in front of me. I could see wet circles under her arms.

"I'm looking for Joy."

"That makes two of us." She wasn't happy. We were standing by the front desk and she grabbed a towel from it, mopped her brow, and then hung it over her shoulders. She was about five four and had to look up at me slightly.

"What do you mean?"

"This was supposed to be her class," she said. "I'm doing a double here."

I decided to play up to her.

"Well, you sure look like you can handle it."

She blinked, smiled, and then said uncertainly, "Well . . . thanks."

"Was she here yesterday?"

"No, not then, either. I called, but there was no answer. You her new boyfriend?"

"No. Why, does she have a new boyfriend?"

She shrugged. "I don't know. I haven't seen Ray around, and now you show up. I was just trying to put two and two together."

In talking to her she began to become more attractive, especially when she smiled.

"Why are you looking for her?"

"I'm looking for Ray. I thought she could tell me where he is."

"She was complaining Tuesday that she hadn't seen him lately."

I nodded.

"You a cop?"

I shook my head. "Private."

"Really?"

I nodded.

"How interesting."

"Helen?"

One of the girls in the class was calling. It was then that both Helen and I noticed that Donna Summers had finished.

"Okay, okay," she said, waving at them. She turned back to me and said, "Sorry I couldn't help you."

"Sorry I interrupted your class."

"No problem. What's your name?"

"Miles Jacoby."

"Helen Scott, Scott and Edelstein Advertising. I'm in the book, business and home."

"I'll remember."

She smiled, transforming her face once again, and then went back to her class. As I left, Janet Jackson started yelling about a "black cat."

Bass on high, of course.

29

THAT WAS WHEN I went to Joy's apartment and found her in the bathtub. . . .

It was confusing for a while. The first officer on the scene looked at me suspiciously. One of them kept an eye on me while the other called the squeal in. Before the detectives arrived, another radio car arrived, and a sergeant's car. The sergeant—wearing a name tag that said Casey—sent two of the uniformed men to canvass the building. He then put one man of the original responding team in the bathroom, and the other one at the front door of the apartment. He and I sat in the kitchen on two undamaged chairs while his driver went downstairs to wait for the squad.

I explained what I was doing there twice before the detectives finally arrived. I was hoping I'd be lucky enough that the team who caught the case would be Pell and his partner, but I didn't know either of the detectives who entered. It didn't help that one of them was a woman.

"Sarge?" one of the detectives said.

"Casey."

"Detective Sandoval. And Detective Yearwood."

Yearwood was the female.

"Who's catchin'?" Casey asked.

"I am," Sandoval said. He was in his mid-thirties, and while his name was Hispanic, he did not look it. His partner, Yearwood, looked to be in her early forties. She had a plain face, no makeup, short hair, and was stockily built but remained decidedly feminine. They had the appearance of a team who had been together awhile, which meant they did not look as hopelessly mismatched as Pell and his partner did.

"What do we have?" he asked.

"A dead girl in the bathtub."

"Was the apartment like this when you got here?"

"Yup."

"Who called it in?"

"This fella," Casey said. "I checked his ID. He's a private badge named Jacoby."

Sandoval looked at me, and then looked closer.

"I know you, don't I?"

I hoped he did.

"Do you?"

"Yes, I'm sure—wait, you were in the office a little while ago, talking with the kid."

"Pell?" his partner asked.

"Yeah." Sandoval looked at his partner. "You were out for coffee. This man came in and talked to Pell."

"About what?" I wasn't sure if Yearwood was asking her partner or me, but I answered.

"A murder."

"This one?"

"No, another one. Last night."

"The comedian, right?" Sandoval asked.

"That's right."

"You found that one last night, and this one today?"

"I didn't find the one last night, I just happened to be in the club when he was found."

"And what about this girl?"

I made it as simple as possible.

"Her boyfriend's a friend of mine. I was looking for him. When I got here, the door was open. I came in, found her, and called you."

"Stay here." He looked at Yearwood and said, "Let's take a look."

I waited under the watchful eye of the sergeant while Sandoval and Yearwood went to take a look at Joy. When they came back they stood in almost the exact spots they had left.

"What's her name?" Sandoval asked.

"Joy White."

"How well did you know her?"

"Not well."

"She was beaten pretty badly from the way it looks."

"I know."

"Let me see your hands."

I held them out so that he could inspect my knuckles.

"No way he could have inflicted that damage without messin' up his own hands."

"What if he didn't use his hands?" Yearwood asked.

"That's a possibility," Sandoval said.

I stayed quiet because I didn't feel they really thought I did it.

At that moment a uniformed officer came to the door and spoke to the sergeant. In turn, he spoke to Sandoval, who then spoke to Yearwood. When all of that was done, they came back to me. I was reminded of a childhood game called "telephone." I wondered how much of what the first officer said had actually reached Yearwood's ears. Oh well, these weren't children.

"How'd you get into the building without a key?" Sandoval asked.

He already knew and wanted to see if I would lie.

"I pressed doorbell buzzers and announced that I was delivering pizza until somebody let me in."

They all stared at me, and then Sandoval said, "Smart."

"Sometimes I use Chinese food," I said. "Not everybody likes pizza."

"I like Chinese food better than pizza, myself," Yearwood said.

"Maybe we better call Pell," Sandoval said.

"Why?" I asked.

"I'd like to cut you loose. Maybe he'll vouch for you."

"I just met him last night."

Sandoval shrugged. "The kid's funny."

"Well, if he doesn't want to vouch for me," I said, "call Detective Hocus, Major Case Squad over in the Seventeenth. He'll vouch for me."

"I know Hocus," Yearwood said.

Sandoval looked at her and said, "Call him."

As his partner went to the phone, Sandoval said to me, "We'll try and get rid of you before the duty captain arrives, or you'll never get out of here."

While he had no accent, I had the feeling that English was not Detective Sandoval's first language; it was too perfect. He said, "before the duty captain arrives" rather than "before he gets here," and he didn't use contractions very much.

"Who is the boyfriend?" he asked me.

"Ray Carbone."

Sandoval frowned. "I know that name."

"Maybe."

"What is his claim to fame?"

"He does odd jobs."

"That's right," Sandoval said, snapping his fingers, "he has been known to bend the law from time to time, right?"

"Bend is right," I lied. "I don't think he's ever really broken it."

"Maybe not until now."

"Ray didn't do that."

"Why not?"

"She was his girl."

"So?"

"Also, he wouldn't touch a woman that way."

"Lots of men beat women, Mr. Jacoby."

"Not Ray."

Sandoval shrugged, and Yearwood returned.

"Did you talk to him?"

"Yeah," Yearwood said, "he vouches for him."

"What do you know about Hocus?" Sandoval asked her.

"He's a good cop. If he says this guy is okay I'd believe him."

"Do you want to cut him loose?"

"We don't need him getting underfoot."

Sandoval looked at me and said, "You can go, but I want you at the precinct tomorrow."

"What time?"

"Four."

"Not earlier?"

Sandoval shrugged.

"You keep finding your bodies on the four to twelve."

"I didn't—" I started to say, then decided to forget it. "Okay, I'll be there. Thanks."

As I headed for the door, Sandoval asked, "Where are you headed?"

"Why?"

"I just wouldn't want you to find any more bodies."

"At least not until the twelve to eight tour starts," Yearwood said.

"I'm going home."

"Good," Sandoval said, "stay there."

I frowned. Was he telling me not to look for Ray anymore?

"Find something to watch on TV," Yearwood said.

"*Quantum Leap*," Sandoval said.

"If he's got cable," Yearwood said.

I looked at Casey, who was staring back and forth between the two partners, a confused look on his face.

"I can take a hint," I assured them, and left.

▽

30

I WENT HOME, but I had no intention of watching TV. First I called Hocus and thanked him for the support.

"Yearwood asked me about the possibility of you beating a girl to death."

"What did you tell her?"

"I told her she never saw you in the ring or she wouldn't be asking me that question."

"You told them I used to be a fighter."

"You forgot."

"They didn't ask me."

"It works in your favor," he said. "It's more likely if you did beat anybody to death you'd use your hands, and from what he told me your hands are unmarked."

"Virgin."

"What's Ray gotten himself into, Jack?"

"I don't know. I'm trying to find out."

"Well, I like Ray as much as the next guy, but don't stick your neck out."

"He's my friend, Hocus."

"Okay, so don't stick it out too far."

"I'll watch it."

"And let me know if you need any help."

"You helped already. Thanks again."

When I hung up on Hocus, I called Heck and told him what had happened.

"This is getting decidedly ugly."

"I want to talk to Pesce, Heck."

"Why?"

"Because I haven't, yet. Because maybe I'll ask him something you didn't think to ask."

"All right," Heck said, taking no offense. "I'll arrange it. Nine A.M."

"I'll be there."

"Jack?"

"Yeah?"

"I'm sorry about the girl."

"Yeah."

I hung up and, just as an afterthought, dialed Ray's number. When I brought up his messages, there were two.

Beep.

"Ray, I heard Joy had an accident. Too bad."

Jesus, the nerve of the guy, whoever he was. Well, this message might help to clear Ray once I told Sandoval about it. I waited, and the second message came up.

Beep.

"Jack, I don't need the help. Stay out of it."

I stared at the phone. That message was from Ray.

Normally, if Ray Carbone ever told me that he didn't need my help I'd back off, but not this time. I had the feeling Ray was into something heavy. Maybe he didn't know he needed help, or just didn't think so, but he was going to get it anyway.

Next I dialed Packy's. I had two phone numbers, one of which I used for my PI business. Geneva, Marty, and Ed all knew not to answer that phone. After the fourth ring, my machine picked up, and after my message I pressed my code and picked up my own messages.

There was just one.

"Mr. Jacoby, this is Andrea Legend. Please call me. It's urgent, so please reply as soon as possible. Thank you." She gave her business number, and home number, and hung up.

Maybe it was urgent, but it wasn't so urgent that she'd drop her business manner.

My telephone work was done, and it was still early. I had

several options. I could go to Packy's and hang out until closing. Or I could check out some more of Ray's hangouts. Or I could go and try to get into Stan Waldrop's apartment. What were my priorities? Both cases now involved murder, and while Ray was my friend, I had taken money from Waldrop.

I decided to try Andrea Legend's home number.

"Hello?"

She had a distinctive voice even while speaking one word.

"Andrea? It's Miles Jacoby."

"Oh." She sounded surprised. "I didn't expect you to call me . . . here."

"You left your home number and said it was urgent."

"I did, of course, I, uh, just didn't expect you to call this late."

"I'm sorry—"

"No, no, actually it's not that late. In fact, if you would like, you could come up here now."

"What's so urgent?"

"Well . . . I wasn't completely honest with you this afternoon."

"About what?"

There was a long hesitation period, and then she said, "I do have a key to Stan's apartment."

I didn't ask her why she had lied.

"Can I have it?"

"Well, yes, of course. Can you come and pick it up tonight?"

"Give me your address."

She rattled it off. It was uptown, on the east side.

"Give me about half an hour." That would get me to her door at about nine.

"Yes, all right. I'll see you then."

I hung up and thought about going uptown to see a beautiful woman in her apartment.

It was better than watching *Quantum Leap*.

31

ANDREA LEGEND'S BUILDING was on East Eighty-first Street between York and First avenues. It was a modern high-rise with a uniformed doorman. He called upstairs for permission to let me in.

"Take the elevator to the eleventh floor, sir. Apartment eleven-fourteen."

"Thanks."

I rode the elevator to eleven, the ride hardly taking any time at all. This was the kind of building Heck should have had his office in so I wouldn't have to ride that slow-moving rattletrap that masqueraded as an elevator in his building.

I walked to 1114 and pressed the doorbell. When she opened the door I thought that if she had dressed so as not to give me any ideas, she had gone the wrong way.

She seemed to be wearing some sort of stay-at-home outfit, a black teddy under a long, black, robe-type thing. I was willing to bet she could have worn it to all kinds of parties and no one would have known it was night wear. It was black, but filmy, very low cut in front to reveal a deep, pale cleavage, and it reached to the floor. It was just tasteful enough so that I couldn't swear she was flaunting it, but sexy enough so that she could claim she was.

"Come in," she said.

I wasn't sure I wanted to.

"Thanks."

I entered, and in moving past her caught a whiff of her perfume. It matched the outfit perfectly. It was appropriate for the office, and yet would not have been out of place in the bedroom.

What was the story here?

I decided the best move was to ask.

"Have I interrupted something?"

She turned from the closed door to face me. Her makeup was perfectly applied, as it had been in her office. Perhaps the only difference would have been a little more blush applied to her cheeks. Still, I had seen her toward the end of the day, and the blush could have rubbed off.

"No. Why would you ask?"

"You seem a little overdressed just to give me a key. I figured you were expecting company."

"No," she said, thinking fast, "no, no one . . . just you. . . ."

"Not dressed like that."

"Why not?" Her tone was defensive.

"Because I'm not on your menu, Andrea. The price is too low."

"I don't understand."

"Sure you do. You thought if you dressed like that and talked sexy I'd fall into bed with you."

"I don't want you—"

"That's true enough. You *don't* want me in your bed, which makes me all the more curious why you'd pull this seduction act."

She stared at me for a few moments until I thought she was going to crack, but then she sucked it up and decided to brazen it out.

"I don't know what you're talking about, Mr. Jacoby." She walked to a small table near the door with an oriental vase on it and picked up a key.

"Here's the key to Stan's apartment."

"Why did you tell me you didn't have one?"

"I . . . forgot."

"Was there anything going on between you and Stan, Andrea?"

"Of course not."

"No little extracurricular bedroom athletics going on?"

"This is insulting."

"What about you and Allegretto? You two looked pretty cozy last night."

"I think it's time for you to leave, Mr. Jacoby."

"What happened, I thought we were on a first-name basis?"

She pulled the front of her outfit closed to hide her cleavage. I got the feeling she was embarrassed about her botched seduction attempt.

"Please leave."

"Thanks for the key, Andrea. If you decide you want to talk—I mean, really talk—give me a call."

She just stood there as I let myself out, her arms crossed over her breasts, staring down at the floor.

In the elevator I wondered what the hell that was all about. First she lies about having a key, then she gets me to come to her apartment to pick it up, planning some sort of seduction scene . . . but for what?

Maybe I should have just kept quiet and waited a little longer before asking her.

32

S TAN WALDROP LIVED in an apartment building on the corner of Eighth Avenue and West Fifty-third Street. While it wasn't in the same class as Andrea's—there was no doorman—it was certainly beyond my price range.

I went inside, took the elevator to the fifth floor, and let myself in with the key. Waldrop's place was on the back side of the building, so his view was of the backs and tops of other buildings. It was a small three-room, one-bedroom place that would have been too cramped for me—especially at a high price. I looked around the living room and kitchen briefly, and then went into his bedroom. There was a small writing desk by the window, with a computer on it. The setup looked to me to be in five pieces. There was the computer, the TV-type monitor, the keyboard, a telephone with another device next to it that I assumed was a modem, and a printer. I stood staring down at it, realizing that there would be no point in my turning it on. I didn't know the first thing to do, and with my luck I'd touch one key and wipe the thing clean.

What I needed was someone who knew computers.

I took another look around, this time opening and closing drawers. In one of the desk drawers I found a stamped and used airline ticket to and from Las Vegas. Apparently, just before hiring me Waldrop had played Vegas. I guessed that it was when he returned from there that he'd discovered the theft of his jokes.

I put the ticket in my pocket and kept looking around. In the living room was another phone with an answering machine connected. There were no new messages waiting for him, but since I had gone to the trouble of taking Ray's tape and playing it back with Geneva's microrecorder, I decided to do the same with Waldrop's. I popped it out of the machine and dropped it in my pocket. I didn't think I needed to bother with replacing it. He wouldn't be getting any new calls.

Just as an afterthought I picked up the phone and dialed Andrea Legend's home number.

"Hello?" She answered after four rings.

"Are you still mad at me?"

There was a moment's hesitation and then she said, "Furious."

Just from the tone of voice in that one word I realized that she had regained her composure.

"Want me to come back?"

"No, I'm afraid it's too late for that."

"I blew it, huh?"

"Decidedly."

"Well, maybe next time."

She didn't reply. Go ahead, make me sweat.

"Listen, Andrea, I need to ask you something about Stan."

"What?"

"Was he in Las Vegas last week?"

"He was."

"And it was when he came back that he discovered someone had stolen his jokes?"

"Yes."

"Where was he playing in Vegas?"

"The Aladdin."

Not top of the line, but not bad either.

"Okay, thanks."

"That's it?"

"That's all. Go back to sleep, or whatever you were doing, with whoever . . ."

"I'm alone."

"Oh."

"There was nothing between Stan and me, Miles."

"Okay, if you say so."

"And there's nothing going on between me and Bill Allegretto."

"Okay."

"I don't sleep with my clients."

"Okay." There was nothing else for me to say.

"You think I'm a cold bitch, don't you?"

"One out of two."

A pause.

"Which one?"

"Guess," I said, and hung up.

Let *her* sweat.

▽

33

At nine the next morning I presented myself at the Tombs in downtown Manhattan. Heck had made the arrangements, and before long I found myself in a room with Danny Pesce sitting across a table from me.

Pesce was tall and slender, with long, lank black hair that looked as if it hadn't been washed in days, maybe longer. He looked to be in his early forties. Instead of looking at me he stared down at his hands, picking skin off the fingers of the left one.

"Danny, I'm Miles Jacoby, an investigator working for your lawyer, Heck Delgado."

"Uh-huh."

"I'm also a friend of Ray Carbone's."

"Did you find him?"

"Not yet."

He looked at me now.

"Ray's gotta come in, man. He can get me off."

"What was Ray's involvement, Danny?"

Pesce shook his head and went back to looking down at his hands. I could see that a couple of fingers had small scabs on them, so apparently he picked at the skin until it bled.

"I ain't sayin'. Not to you, anyway."

"Talking to me is like talking to your lawyer."

"I ain't told him, either."

"Why not?"

"I'm a stand-up guy, man. I ain't rattin' Ray. He's gotta come in on his own."

"And if he doesn't?"

"I know what I'm gonna do if that happens."

"You're going to give him up?"

Pesce didn't answer.

"You know, if you wait any longer nobody's going to believe you."

"Nobody believes me now that I didn't kill nobody. They'll believe me, though, when Ray comes in. He's my witness."

"Is that all he is, Danny? A witness? If so, why's he on the run?"

"I ain't sayin'."

Danny Pesce was small-time, but it had been drilled into him since childhood that you didn't rat anybody out—not if you could help it. I had no doubt that if the time came for him to go to trial, and Ray hadn't turned up, he'd give Ray up—but for what?

"Danny, did Ray kill Michael Bonetti?"

Pesce shook his head stubbornly and said, "I ain't sayin'." He pulled a stubborn piece of skin off his thumb and a small bead of blood immediately appeared. He put the thumb into his mouth.

"Okay, then help me find Ray, Danny. Where can I look for him?"

"You said you was his friend."

"I am. I checked some of the places he goes to, I checked his apartment."

"Check with Joy."

"I did." I watched him carefully. "I saw her once, and then when I went to see her again she was dead."

His head came up, and his thumb popped out of his mouth with a wet sound.

"What?"

"Joy's dead."

"How?"

"Somebody beat her to death, just like Michael Bonetti."

"Oh, Jesus . . ."

"Tell me something that will help me help you, Danny."

"I got nothin' to tell you." He spread his hands helplessly. "All I can tell you is you gotta find Ray. Ray's gotta come in and clear me."

"Danny, even if I find Ray there's no guarantee he's going to come in."

"He's my witness, man, he's gotta come in."

"Will coming in and talking incriminate him? Because if it will, he probably won't do it."

Pesce suddenly slammed both of his hands down on the table and stood up.

"You gotta find him, man. You gotta! That's all I can tell you."

"All right, Danny, all right. I'll keep trying."

I ran into Heck outside.

"Here to see him?"

Heck shook his head.

"Another client, but I thought I'd check in with you. Anything?"

"He wouldn't—or couldn't—give me anything that would help me find Ray. He wouldn't even tell me exactly what Ray had to do with the murder."

"I'll talk to him again," Heck said, "but he's been taught since he was a child—"

"I know, you don't rat anybody out. Be a stand-up guy."

"It's important to men like him."

"Yeah, maybe," I said, "but only up to a point."

We separated and I went outside. What was it that was making Danny Pesce keep silent? Was he just being a stand-up guy, or was he afraid of something? Or somebody? And what about Joy? What did her death have to do with Bonetti's death?

And where the hell was Ray Carbone?

$\triangledown$

34

THAT MORNING I got to Packy's even before Geneva did. When I went into the office, I saw a Federal Express envelope on the desk. It must have been delivered the day before and Geneva had left it there. When I sat at the desk and looked at it, I saw that the sender was Walker Blue.

I slit open the envelope and took out a brown nine-by-twelve envelope. Inside that I found the partnership papers Walker had drawn up. I left them on the desk without reading them. I wasn't in the mood to wade through pages and pages of legalese this morning.

I leaned back in my chair and took Geneva's little tape recorder out of my pocket, along with the two tapes—the one from Ray's machine and the one from Stan Waldrop's machine. I laid the machine on the desk with a tape on either side. I doubted that I'd be working either case if Walker and I had become partners a month earlier. Stan Waldrop certainly wouldn't have gone to Walker Blue Associates, and Heck probably would have hired someone else as well, even though he knew I was friends with Ray Carbone. No, that wasn't right. Heck would have called me—at least I hoped he would have called.

Wait a minute. Thinking back to that initial interview with Truman Tyler in Heck's office, hadn't either he or Heck said that Pesce sent him to find both Heck and me? Damn it. I'd had the chance that morning to ask Pesce why he asked for me, and I'd blown it. How had he known that I was friends with Ray? Had Ray mentioned me to him often enough for him to remember when he was arrested?

And what about Truman Tyler? I hadn't talked to him since that afternoon in Heck's office. Maybe he knew more than he was saying. After all, hadn't he left three messages on Ray's machine? Why was he trying to find Ray on his own before coming to Heck and me?

I put Walker's partnership papers back in the envelope and tucked them away in the top desk drawer. I put the recorder and the two tapes back into the pockets of my jacket. Then I pulled the Yellow Pages out of the bottom right-hand drawer and looked up Truman Tyler under "Attorneys." When I didn't find him, I tried finding a listing for "Lawyers" but that only said to see "Attorneys."

Tyler wasn't listed.

I put the phone book away and called Missy.

"Heck's not here, Miles."

"I know, Missy, I saw him this morning. When Truman Tyler was there the other day, did he leave an address and phone number?"

"Sure, hold on."

She came back in a moment and gave me both. I thanked her and hung up, feeling stupid. The reason Tyler wasn't listed in the Manhattan Yellow Pages was because his office was in Brooklyn.

Did I want to go to Brooklyn to talk to him? I guess I didn't have much choice, but before doing that I called a friend of mine in Brooklyn, Nick Delvecchio.

Delvecchio's real godfather, Dominick Barracondi—otherwise known as "Nicky Barracuda"—was the supposedly retired godfather of Brooklyn, now choosing to spend his days running his Italian restaurant in Sheepshead Bay. With his connections I figured maybe he would have some info on Tyler.

Luckily, he was in when I called.

"What can I do for you, Miles? If I remember correctly I still owe you a few."

"I don't know who owes who, Nick, but I do need to pick your brain a little."

"Go ahead."

"You know a lawyer named Truman Tyler, with an office on Court Street?"

"Just barely on Court Street," he corrected me. "He's got a Court Street address, but it's actually a door around the side of the building, over a deli."

"He's that small-time?"

"That small-time. Is this about Danny Pesce?"

"How do you know about that?"

"I read the papers, Miles."

"Do you know Pesce?"

"I've run across him once or twice."

I frowned. "Is he from Brooklyn too?"

"He is."

"What the hell are Pesce and Tyler doing in Manhattan?" I asked out loud.

"I understand some people cross the bridge from time to time, Miles."

"Unlike you, huh?"

"You want me to nose around a little? Maybe find out why Pesce was having dealings with a Manhattan bookie like Bonetti?"

"Did you know Bonetti?"

"No, never met him or heard of him until I read the papers. How'd you get involved in this, Jack?"

"Pesce wants me to find Ray Carbone."

Delvecchio knew Ray.

"What's Carbone got to do with it?"

"Pesce seems to think Ray can clear him."

"Does he say Ray did it?"

"He's not saying anything, but that I have to find Ray."

"And that's proving to be a problem?"

"A big one." I decided not to elaborate. I really didn't want to drag Nick into the case, I simply wanted to pick his brain.

"What's Tyler's claim to fame, Nick? He doesn't exactly have an Italian name."

"His mother's Italian, his father was Jewish."

"What a combination. Was his mother, uh, connected to anybody?"

"I don't know, but I can ask around."

"Don't get into trouble because of it."

"That's not a problem."

"Okay, then do it." I still kept him in the dark about Joy, and some of the other facts. He was just going to ask some questions for me.

"I'll get back to you when I know something."

"Thanks, Nick."

"Hey, Jack?"

"What?"

"You crossing the bridge?"

"Yeah, probably."

"Want me to get you a bodyguard to meet you on this side?"

"I want you to get bent," I said, and hung up on his laughter.

▽

35

W HEN GENEVA CAME to work she exhibited what was becoming her customary surprise at finding me there early.

"I won't be here for long," I assured her, "I've got work to do."

"Like the rest of us don't?"

"Speaking of the rest of you, tell Marty I'm going to need him to help me with some computer stuff."

"Is he gonna make overtime?"

"Is he asking, or you?"

"Both."

"Tell him he's going to do me a favor."

"When?"

"Tonight. Get him to stay around."

"For free? How do I do that?"

"Use your considerable charm, my love."

"I hope that ain't an example of yours," she said as I went out the door.

I took the BMT line across the bridge and got off at Court Street. I could count on one hand the times I'd been to Brooklyn, but the last time had been fairly recently. Delvecchio had been working two cases a while back and had needed somebody to tail the husband of a client. I'd helped out some, but hadn't been back until now.

Court Street reminded me of a dirtier, smaller Manhattan block. I walked past a combination Dunkin' Donuts, Nathan's, and Roy Rogers' on my way to finding Truman

Tyler's address. Most of the high-rises on this street house lawyers' offices. In fact, if this part of Court Street was ever blown up by terrorists, the legal profession in Brooklyn would be almost wiped out.

I hadn't called ahead for fear that Tyler would arrange not to be in when I arrived. I wanted to surprise him. Of course, there was always the chance he'd be in court, but I had the feeling that Tyler was the kind of lawyer who tried to settle everything out of court.

I saw what Delvecchio had meant when I found the number I was looking for. The address was on the door of a deli, but around the side was a black metal staircase that led up to the second floor. There was a window overlooking the front of the deli that said TRUMAN TYLER, ATTORNEY-AT-LAW, and the same thing was written on the door. As I entered, I found myself in a small waiting room with an empty desk, a tacky vinyl sofa, and magazines that were months old. The desk was dusty, so I guessed that Tyler had not had a secretary or receptionist for some time.

The door to the inner office was open, and I stepped to it and looked inside. Truman Tyler had his back to me and was going through a file drawer looking for something.

"Secretary's day off?" I asked.

He whirled around, his eyes wide with fright, slamming the drawer as he did.

"Jesus!" he said. "You scared me."

"Nice office, Truman. Not top of the line, but . . ."

"What do you want?"

He wasn't as polite as he had been in Heck's office, but then neither was I.

"Mind if I sit?"

He thought it over and then waved a hand at the cheap plastic chair he was using for visitors. He sat down behind his desk and studied me warily.

"Have you found Carbone?" he asked when I didn't speak right away.

"I haven't, but I found his girlfriend."

That made him frown.

"We weren't looking for his—"

"She's dead."

After a moment he said, "What?"

"Beaten to death. Does that sound familiar?"

He squirmed in his chair.

"That means that Danny couldn't have killed Bonetti."

"No," I said, "you're jumping to conclusions. All this means is that he couldn't have killed the girl because he's in the lockup."

"Carbone could have done it."

"Why would Ray beat his own girlfriend to death?"

"I don't know. I'm just saying it's a possibility. All I'd have to prove to a jury is that there's a possibility that someone else could have done it."

"You? I thought Heck Delgado would be taking this case to trial."

"Well, yes, he will, but . . . I was just saying."

"Truman, tell me why you left three messages for Ray Carbone on his telephone answering machine before you came looking for Heck and me?"

"I didn't."

I took out Geneva's recorder and Ray's tape.

"Want me to play them back?"

Tyler closed his eyes.

"No. I just thought maybe if I could find him, Danny would let me work the case."

"You want to work this case yourself?"

"Of course. I'm a good lawyer."

I made a point of looking around his office.

"Okay, so I don't have a Fifth Avenue office, but that doesn't mean I'm not good."

"I'm not buying that as a reason, Truman."

"Why not?"

"Because I think you're too smart to really think you're a good lawyer. No, I think there's something going on here that Heck and I don't know about. You and Pesce were into something, and you brought Ray into it. When all hell broke loose and Pesce got tagged with Bonetti's murder, you decided you needed to find Ray. Carbone must have mentioned me, and that I sometimes did work for Heck Delgado, so you guys decided to kill two birds with one stone—hire a top attorney, and get me to find Ray Carbone."

Tyler didn't say a word.

"What are you into, Truman?"

He didn't answer.

"I talked to Danny today."

"So?"

"He's keeping his mouth shut, but once it looks like he's going to go up for Bonetti's murder do you think he'll stay quiet? He'll give Ray up, he'll give you up . . . hell, he'd give his mother up. Danny Pesce doesn't exactly strike me as a prime example of a stand-up guy, Truman. Does he give you that impression?"

No answer. I hadn't gotten anywhere with Pesce, and I wasn't getting anywhere with Tyler, but maybe I was planting some seeds.

"Think about it, Truman," I said, standing up. "Ray's on the run from somebody. How long will it be before they come after you?"

Tyler was sweating, but he still wasn't talking. I took out my business card and dropped it on his desk.

"When things get really hot, call me or Heck. Maybe we'll still be able to help you. Maybe."

▽

36

I WAS HAPPY to get back to Manhattan. Brooklyn doesn't impress me. How can you be impressed with a city that had a baseball team—a good baseball team—and lost it? Okay, so New York lost the Giants, but we replaced them with the Mets. We still have *two* teams. How many does Brooklyn have?

None.

I rest my case. (I know, I know, the Yanks play in the Bronx and the Mets in Queens. Technically speaking, *Manhattan* doesn't have a team, but at least we never lost one.)

I was satisfied that I had hit pay dirt. Tyler and Pesce were into something together, some kind of scam. I'd hate to think that Ray was in it with them, but it was possible. If he'd seen a way to make some big money, he might have gone for it.

Because the dead man was a bookie, the scam would have to have had something to do with gambling. However, the dead man was a Manhattan bookie, and both Pesce and Tyler were Brooklyn boys. They probably would have needed somebody to bring them together with Bonetti . . . and whether I liked it or not, that could have been Ray Carbone.

When I got back to Packy's, Geneva told me that Marty wasn't there yet. "He's not really due until three."

"Fine."

I went into the office and saw the red light flashing on my answering machine.

Beep.

"Mr. Jacoby, this is Detective Sandoval from the Sixth. I

have some information you might be interested in. Please give me a call. I'll be in early today, from eleven to seven."

Before the tape had a chance to rewind, I had dialed the Sixth and asked for the squad.

The man who answered said "Squad" but did not identify himself as a detective. He might have been a civilian employee.

"Detective Sandoval, please."

"One moment."

I waited and counted. Sandoval came on before I reached ten.

"This is Sandoval."

"Jacoby here. Thanks for your call."

"I thought you'd be interested to know that the woman wasn't just beaten, she was tortured."

"What?"

"The ME found cigarette burns on her breasts, her pubes, and the soles of her feet. We don't know in what order they were administered."

I didn't think I'd ever heard anyone say "pubes" before. Another cop—like Pell's partner, Matthews—would have said "cunt," or something of that nature.

"So whoever killed her was looking for something."

"And thought she knew where it was."

"I wonder if she did. I wonder if she told him."

"What about you?"

"What about me?"

"Think you might know what they were looking for?"

"I haven't got a clue, Detective."

"Maybe they were just looking for your friend Carbone."

"That could be."

"Any luck with that yet?"

"No."

"Would you tell me if you had found him?"

"Yes."

"How about telling me why you're looking for him in the first place?"

"I don't know if I can."

"You working for a lawyer?"

"Yes."

"So we're dealing with client confidentiality."

"Yes."

"Talk to your lawyer, Jacoby. I'd like to know if the reason you're looking for Carbone could be connected with his girlfriend's death, huh?"

"Okay."

"I gave you a little, right?"

"Right."

"Now you give me a little back."

"That's how it works."

"Let's remember that."

"I'll be in touch, Detective. Uh, I guess you don't need to see me this afternoon, right?"

"No, but if you don't stay in touch . . ."

We hung up and I called Heck right away.

"He's in court, Miles," Missy said.

"Have him call me when he gets in, okay, Missy? I need a clarification on what I can and can't tell the police who are working on Joy's murder."

"All right."

I hung up and sat back in my chair and then decided I needed a beer. I went behind the bar and got myself an Icehouse. People hadn't discovered it yet. The Buds and Millers and Rolling Rocks were going, but not the Icehouse. I didn't mind. I liked it.

"Drinking up the profits?" Geneva asked. She was working on a glass of club soda. I had never seen her take a drink while working behind the bar.

"I need it. I got some news about Ray Carbone's girl-friend."

"Like what?"

"Like you don't want to know, Gen."

"I ever meet her?"

"I think she was in here once with Ray."

"Blond hair, right? Like real blond, but dark eyebrows? Real fit?"

"She was an aerobics instructor."

"I remember her. Somebody did somethin' bad to her, huh?"

"Pretty bad," I said, and took a swig of the beer.

"You gettin' any closer to findin' him?"

"No."

"What about the joke man's jokes?"

"Not that, either."

"What's happenin' with the partnership?"

"I got the papers, but I haven't read them."

"Decide what you're gonna do with us?"

"With this place, you mean? No."

"We part of this place, Boss. You dump it, you dump us."

"That's not fair, Gen. I haven't thought it through. I have too much on my mind right now."

"We can wait."

A customer came in and sat at the bar and she went to see what he wanted. Marty was still about an hour away from coming in, and I didn't know what Ed's schedule was. I left all of that to Geneva.

I took another beer and carried it and the one I was working on back into the office.

▽

37

Marty came in at three sharp, on time for a change. Before he'd arrived I'd asked Geneva where Ed was.

"Got the day off."

"Why did you give him the day off?"

"He asked for it."

"I need to use Marty away from the bar, Gen."

"Well, I didn't know that when I gave Ed the day off, did I?"

"Well, how am I going to take Marty—"

"I can handle it here until it gets busy. Just have him back by six."

Actually, I figured I'd probably have him back before then.

"You white men, you make a big deal out of everything."

"Hey, hey, no racist remarks in my bar."

"That wasn't a racist remark, it was an observation based on fact."

"Well . . . none of that, either."

When Marty came in I told him not to bother getting behind the bar.

"Why not?"

"I need you for something else."

"Like what?"

"I'll tell you on the way."

We caught a cab outside, and I gave the driver the address of Stan Waldrop's building. By the time we arrived, I had explained to Marty what I wanted him to do.

"Can you do it?" I asked as we got out of the cab.

"I can get in there and snoop around, Boss, but a lot will depend on the program he had and whether or not he used passwords."

"Passwords?" We got into the elevator. "What do passwords have to do with anything?"

"If he labeled his files and used passwords, I won't be able to get anywhere without them."

"That's just great."

"From what you told me, though, somebody got into his machine and stole something. They couldn't have done that if he had a password for the file."

"That's good." "Unless he had a password, and they knew it."

"That's bad."

We got out of the elevator, and I let us into Waldrop's apartment.

"It's in the bedroom."

"Am I getting overtime for this?"

"You're doing me a favor, which I'll keep in mind when it comes time for holiday bonuses."

"We didn't get a holiday bonus last year."

"That's what I'll keep in mind."

We went into the bedroom, and I watched as he sat down in front of the computer and turned it on. Already he'd done something I probably couldn't have done without him.

"Okay," he said, staring at the screen, "he's got Windows, Microsoft Word for Windows, he's got WordPerfect for Windows . . ."

He continued to mutter like that, and he might as well have been speaking a foreign language for all the sense it made to me.

". . . Prodigy, Quickstart, Quicken . . ."

Yeah, I thought, Framus, Remus, and Thingamajig.

"Let's try this . . . what am I looking for, Boss?"

"A file with jokes?" I said. "Or maybe a file that used to have jokes in it, but doesn't anymore."

He turned around and looked at me.

"If someone stole the file it won't be here. If they duplicated it, then it would still be here."

"Wait," I said. "Somebody could have duplicated the file?"

"Sure."

"Is there any way to tell when that's been done?"

"No. If they make a copy, there's nothing left behind to indicate that it was done."

"Wait, wait . . . I want to get this straight. If someone is knowledgeable enough to tap into his computer and steal a file, why wouldn't they just copy it so that he wouldn't know it was gone?"

"I don't know."

I didn't expect him to know.

"Keep working, I'm just talking out loud."

Much the way he was as he continued to do what he was doing. With both of us muttering, nothing much was going to get done.

"I'll be in the other room."

"Fine."

"Will it bother you if I use the phone?"

"No."

I went into the other room and sat on the sofa. Maybe whoever stole the joke file wanted Waldrop to know about it. Maybe the point wasn't to steal his jokes for their own use, but simply to drive him crazy and ruin his act.

But why?

I dialed Andrea's work number and she picked up on the second ring.

"It's Miles."

"Well, hello, I—"

"I'm at Stan's, and I've got some questions. Do you have a few minutes?"

"Well, yes—"

"Do you know who Stan's friends were?"

"He didn't have many—"

"I need one or two."

"Why?"

"I just want to talk to someone who knew him, preferably someone in the same business."

"Well, there's Sam Friedlander."

"Who's that?"

"He was Stan's mentor. He used to work the Catskills as Sammy Freed."

I frowned. The name sounded familiar, but I wasn't sure.

"He's retired now."

"Where can I find him?"

"He's usually either at home or at the Stage Deli having lunch."

"Okay."

"Or at Wolf's, or the New York Deli . . ."

"Where else?"

"Maybe the Carnegie."

"I get it, the guy eats deli."

"Every day."

"What's he look like?"

"Well . . . he's in his sixties and wears a really bad rug. It's dark, and the fringe of hair he does have is white. You can't miss him."

"And where does he live?"

She gave me his address.

"Okay, who else? Preferably somebody his own age."

She took a moment to think.

"Well, there's Lenny James."

"Another comic?"

"Yes."

"Do you handle him?"

"No."

"Why not?"

"We don't think he's funny."

"Does he make a living at it?"

"No."

"Okay, where can I find him?"

"I don't know where he lives, but he works as a waiter in

a restaurant on Nineteenth Street, between Sixth and Seventh. Uh, it's called The Rodeo."

"Country and Western?"

"With a name like that, what else?"

"Describe him."

"He's sort of a cross between Larry Fine from the Three Stooges and that guy that plays Kramer on *Seinfeld*."

"I think I'd be able to pick him out. Andrea, how good was Stan with his computer?"

"I don't know."

"How long did he have it?"

"Not long. He only recently decided to use one for his jokes, and his correspondence, and I think his schedule."

"Do you know anyone who would want to ruin Stan's act?"

"A lot of people, Miles. Stan wasn't what you'd call a nice man. He thought he was more successful than he actually was. He had an attitude that pissed off other performers."

I started a little when she said "pissed off." It wasn't a phrase I would have associated with her.

I was going to ask her for some names, but decided not to put her in that position. I wasn't too sure I trusted Andrea, not after what had happened last night. There wasn't really any way she could hide his friends from me, but she didn't have to give me the names of any of Waldrop's enemies—especially if they were clients of hers. I could probably get those names from Friedlander or James.

I thanked her for the information and hung up even though she sounded like she wanted to talk some more.

Once I hung up I decided that I didn't need to stay in the apartment with Marty while he worked.

"Marty, see what you can find for me between now and five, and then head back to the store. Geneva's going to need you for tonight."

"Okay, Boss. If it doesn't take that long, okay if I head back early?"

"Yeah, sure."

"I hope I find something for you. If I do, I'll make a hard copy for you."

"A what?"

He pointed to the printer and said, "I'll print it out."

"Why didn't you say so?"

I went out the door thinking that with all the foreign language we had to deal within this country somebody had to come up with computerese.

▽

38

I WENT TO the address Andrea had given me for Sam Friedlander, also known as Sammy Freed. It was an apartment building on the corner of Fifty-sixth Street and Seventh Avenue, with a doorman. Apparently, Friedlander was able to live comfortably in his retirement.

"I'd like to see Mr. Friedlander."

"Sammy Freed," the doorman said.

"Excuse me?"

"Everybody around here calls him Sammy Freed."

"Okay," I said, "I'd like to see Sammy Freed."

"He ain't here."

"Where is he?"

"We're not supposed to talk about our tenants."

The doorman was in his thirties, a red-haired man who looked ill at ease in his uniform. He was standing behind a little stand, his hands clasped behind his back, and he rocked back on his heels slightly.

Body language.

I took out my wallet and extracted a twenty. It disappeared quickly behind the stand.

"He's still at lunch."

"Which deli?"

"Wolf's today. Corner of—"

"I know where it is," I said. "I wouldn't want to pay extra for something I already know."

"Hey, buddy," he said, "everybody's gotta make a livin', ya know?"

"Yeah, I know."

I started for the door, and he called out, "I'll **give** you something for free."

"Like what?"

"If you want him to talk to you, laugh at his jokes, no matter how old, or how bad—and tell him you remember him. He loves that."

"Thanks, I will."

Wolf's is on the corner of Fifty-seventh and Seventh Avenue. I'd eaten there once or twice. Right across the street is the more ostentatious New York Deli, with its huge front windows strung with whole cuts of meat, and decorated with bottled pickles and peppers. I had eaten there a few times too, mostly when clients wanted to. Once upon a time the place had been an Automat, so it's big, light, and airy.

Wolf's was different. The ceiling was low, and there are different rooms, almost like tunnels, that can't be seen from the front. It was my understanding that Wolf's and the New York Deli are owned by the same people; what counted was that the food was good.

Inside I stopped a waitress as she was going by at high speed.

"Take a table—" she started.

"I'm looking for someone."

"So look—"

"Sam Friedlander."

That stopped her, and she smiled.

"Sammy Freed. He's in the back room, that way." She pointed.

"Thanks."

"You want somethin'?"

"Bring me a brisket on a kaiser, with some fries, and a Doctor Brown's cream soda."

Like I said, I'd eaten there before.

* * *

Andrea had been right about Sammy Freed. I couldn't miss
him. Not only was the rug he was wearing a bad one, but it
was on crooked. He was a comedian, though—at least, he
used to be—maybe he meant to wear it that way.

As I approached his table he was telling two waitresses
and a busboy a joke. They were smiling, but the people
seated at tables around him weren't because they were
waiting for service. It was after three, but Wolf's was still
going strong.

". . . so the monkey says, 'sure . . . now!' "

The busboy and waitresses cracked up and went back to
their jobs.

"Mr. Friedlander?"

The man looked up from his table. He was still smiling
at his own joke and I could see that his false teeth were
stained yellow. He looked about seventy, but I was willing to
bet he was even older.

"The name's Freed, lad, Sammy Freed."

"Sorry," I said. "Mr. Freed, my name's Miles Jacoby."

"Jacoby?" he asked. "Not Ja-co-bee?"

"No, sir," I said. "It's spelled the same, but pronounced
different."

He frowned.

"There's got to be a joke in there someplace."

"Can I sit down?"

"That depends."

"On what?"

"On whether you remember me or not?"

"Well, sure I do. You're Sammy Freed, King of the
Catskills."

Freed laughed and said, "You're good, son, but you went
a little overboard. What can I do for you?"

"I want to talk to you about Stan Waldrop."

"Stanley?" The old man frowned. "What do you know
about Stanley?"

"I was working for him when he died."

"Sit," Freed said. "You want somethin' to eat?"

"I already ordered."

"So confident, you were, that I'd ask you to sit?"

"I hoped."

"All right, then, sit and talk to an old man."

▽

39

FREED HAD A plate in front of him with one bite left of a corned beef on rye, and a few stray french fries. There were two little plastic cups that had been filled with coleslaw, only now they were empty.

The waitress came with my sandwich and fries and soda. She put the plate down and smiled at Freed.

"You want coffee, Sammy?"

"Yeah, Cora, coffee."

As Cora walked away, Freed pointed to the coleslaw on my plate and asked, "You gonna eat that?"

"No," I lied, "I don't like coleslaw."

"I love coleslaw," he said, plucking it off my plate with a liver-spotted hand. "So, tell me about Stanley."

"That's what I want you to do, Mr. Freed."

"Sammy," he said, "you'll call me Sammy, and I'll call you ...."?

"Jack."

"Jack," he said, nodding shortly. "Okay, Jack, first you'll tell me and then I'll tell you, *nu*?"

"What do you want me to tell you, Mist—uh, Sammy?"

"What were you doing for Stanley?"

"I was looking for his jokes."

"His jokes?"

"Somebody stole them from his computer."

"In a computer, he put them? I knew he was all the time writing them down, but in a computer? *Oy*, what's this business coming to? You know, I was never a stand-up comic, I was a comedian. Back when I was working we were all comedians. Mort Sahl, Morty Gunty, Jackie Leonard, we were all comedians. Joey Bishop, he was a comedian. Today, they're stand-up comics? Go figure."

"You never wrote your jokes down, Sammy?"

"Never, not once." There was a spot of white at the corner of his mouth from the coleslaw. I didn't mention it. I bit into my sandwich and waited.

"Stanley, he always had a bad memory, even as a kid."

"You knew him as a kid?"

"I shouldn't know my own nephew? My sister's oldest boy?"

"Stan Waldrop was your nephew."

"Stanley Waldropsky, that was his name when he was growing up. Me, I wanted him to call himself Stanley Wall, but the kid, he wanted to pick his own name. So, he became Stan Waldrop."

"He wanted to be like you, right?"

"You're smart," he said, pointing at me with a fork, "I like that—but you're also a wise guy."

It took me a moment to realize that he didn't mean that in the Italian sense of the word.

"I beg your pardon?"

"You didn't finish telling me what you were doing for Stanley."

"I'm a private investigator. He hired me to find his jokes, but before I could do a thing he was dead."

"I know he's dead," Freed said, sadly, "of that you don't have to remind me."

"Sorry."

"A bang on the back of the head and boom, he's gone. The police don't even know who did it."

"I know."

"Hey, you're a detective, why don't you find out who did it?"

"It's an active police investigation, Sammy. I can't interfere. I'd lose my license."

We paused while the waitress, Cora, filled his coffee cup.

"So, why are you interested in my nephew, then?"

"He paid me for a few days in advance. I want to earn my money."

"Honest? You're honest?" He feigned shock.

"I try to be."

"What do you want to know, then, Mr. Honest Jack, about my nephew who I loved?"

Before answering, I swallowed the bit of sandwich that was in my mouth. Freed started swiping fries from my plate.

"Who wanted him dead?"

"Who knew him?"

"I'm sorry?"

"Stanley was my sister's boy and I loved him, but he was a putz."

"How so?"

"He wanted to make people laugh, but he didn't want people as friends. That's what kept him from being good."

"Could you explain that to me?"

"An audience can feel when you don't like them. Why should they laugh at you if you don't like them? Don Rickles, he insulted his audience, right?"

"Right."

"But he was a good man, he loved people. It was all an act and the people knew it. 'Hockey pucks,' he called them. You know who gave him that?"

"Uh, no—"

"Me," Freed said proudly. "He came to me and I gave him 'hockey pucks'."

"Really?"

"I should lie?"

"No, no, I believe you."

"You should believe me. Sammy Freed doesn't lie. What was I talking about?"

"Stanley the putz."

"Right. So Stanley was a shit. I hate to say it, but it's true. He was the last family I had left, but he was shitty to people."

"Audiences?"

"Everybody. Other comics. They hated him."

"So they hated him?"

"Some of them did. Some of them just didn't like him."

"So how many of them hated him enough to kill him?"

"Kill him because he had a big mouth? That's crazy."

"Somebody killed him, Sammy."

"Not because he had a big mouth and was shitty. There had to be another reason."

"Like what?"

"I should know? You're the big-shot detective. Find out."

"I want to talk to somebody who was Stan's friend."

"Stanley had one friend."

"Who?"

"Lenny James."

I was glad to hear him come up with the same name Andrea had given me.

"Stan's agent told me about James. Were he and your nephew close?"

"Close, shmose, Lenny thought Stan was gonna help him break in."

"And was he?'

"You ask me," Freed said, "there was something else going on there."

"Like what?"

"I should speak ill of the dead? My sister's boy?"

"It might help me, Sammy."

Freed looked pained and stole my last french fry. I had wolfed down the sandwich—no pun intended—or he might have gotten a piece of that too.

"I think maybe my nephew didn't like women."

"What? You mean you think Lenny James and your nephew were—"

"Funny," Freed said, cutting me off, "and I don't mean 'ha-ha'."

I sat back, stunned. I hadn't gotten a sense of that from Waldrop at all.

"Did you hear about the two fags who go into a bar together," Freed said, "the bartender says, 'I don't serve fags.' The first fag says, 'I'm not a fag, I'm gay.' The bartender looks at the second guy and asks, 'What about you?' The second fag says, 'I'll have the same as my gay friend'."

He stopped there and I caught myself still waiting for the punch line.

"See? That was Stan's."

"He wrote that?"

"Yeah. It's shit, right? I didn't do jokes about homosexuals. I never did."

"But Stan did."

"Stanley did jokes about everything. He thought he was the white—what's his name? The black guy?"

"Cosby?"

"No . . ."

"Pryor?"

"No . . ."

"Eddie Murphy?"

"That's him! Eddie Murphy. You know, he might be the only young comic I like, today."

"He does gay jokes."

"Yeah, but good ones." He stopped and looked past me. "Cora? Another cup of coffee. You?" he said to me.

"Oh, yeah."

"Two."

Cora came over with a second cup, put it down, and then filled both.

"So, Sammy, you have no idea who killed your nephew?"

"I should make a list? It would take forever. These young comics he worked with, they hated him."

"Do you know a man named Bill Allegretto?"

"Never heard of him. Is he a comic?"

"Yes."

"Then he hated Stanley."

"Do you know Stan's agent?"

"That big shot with the three-piece suit?"

"A woman who works for him, Andrea Legend."

"Legend? That's a name? Wait a minute, a pretty girl with dark hair, big bubbies out to here?"

"That's her."

"She was his agent?"

"She was handling him, yeah."

"Ah, I saw them together once and I hoped I was wrong about—well, you know."

"I know."

Sure . . . now!

▽

40

I FELT BAD as I left Sammy Freed at Wolf's. He'd been a lonely man before, spending his afternoons telling jokes to waitresses and busboys at delis, and that was before his nephew—his last living relative—was killed. I wondered what it was like to be Freed's age and have outlived all your relatives.

What was I thinking? I was half his age, and I'd already outlived all my relatives.

Boy, now I was really depressed.

Lenny James was next. I took a cab down to Nineteenth Street to The Rodeo, which was right down the block from the big Barnes & Noble bookstore. As I got out of the cab I felt sort of guilty that I wasn't looking for Ray, but I knew Ray Carbone as well as anyone. If he didn't want to be found, there was little chance that I'd find him. Then again, since I did know him well, if anyone could have found him, it should have been me.

Well, Lenny James was right in front of me. First things first.

I went inside and looked around. It was a huge place with enough space between tables to walk a horse. Unusual for a Manhattan restaurant, where they usually crammed tables as close together as possible.

The lunch rush was over, so only a few tables were taken. This was a good time to go to a restaurant if all you wanted was to talk to one of the waiters.

"Can I help you?" one asked as I was looking around for someone who matched James's description.

He was wearing a cowboy hat and a red bandanna, his only concession to working in a Country and Western restaurant. Other than that he wore a white shirt and black pants he could have worn to any other job. He was average height, blond and very slender, in his twenties.

"I'm looking for one of your waiters."

"Which one?"

"Lenny."

He frowned.

"We don't have a waiter named Lenny that I know of."

"Big tall guy, lot of hair?"

"Oh, him."

"Lenny, right?"

"Well, yes, but he's not a waiter."

"Oh?"

"He's a busboy."

"Well, whatever he is, can I talk to him?"

"I'll get him. You wanna sit?"

"Sure."

"Take any table."

I sat down and waited. Before long the waiter returned with a tall man in tow. Andrea's description of James was right on the money, as had been the case with Sammy Freed. This guy looked like a tall, skinny Larry Fine. He wasn't wearing a bandanna or a hat, but then he wasn't a waiter. He had on jeans and a T-shirt.

"Can I help you?" James asked.

I thanked the waiter and he faded away.

"You can if your name is Lenny James."

"That's me. You an agent?"

"What?"

"An agent, a talent agent?"

"No, Lenny, my name is Miles Jacoby. I'm a private investigator."

"Oh." He looked crestfallen. "I thought maybe you caught my act last night."

"No. I'm working for Stan Waldrop."

Now he frowned. "Stan's dead."

"He hired me before he died. Listen, why don't you sit down?"

He looked around a little nervously, maybe afraid he'd get fired.

"Just a few minutes."

"Well, okay," he said, "but you better buy something."

"I'll have a beer."

"What kind?"

"I don't care."

"Have a Lone Star."

"Fine."

James waved the waiter back over and ordered.

"What did Stan hire you to do?"

"He said somebody stole his jokes."

"His jokes?"

I nodded. "Out of his computer."

"He did that?"

"What?"

"He told me he was gonna put all his jokes on computer. I told him I didn't think it was a good idea."

"Why not?"

"He could lose them that way."

"I guess he did."

"No, I didn't mean stolen, I meant that they could be wiped out. I told him to keep a hard copy, but he thought that could be stolen."

Hard copy. I knew what that meant, this time.

"Why was he worried about somebody stealing his jokes?"

"I don't know. He was paranoid. He always thought somebody was going to steal his act and make it big with it."

"Was his act good?"

"It's okay—I mean, it was okay."

"I heard you and him were good friends." I watched his face carefully.

"Yeah, we were tight."

The waiter came with my beer; I declined a glass and took the cold bottle from him.

"You know anybody who might want to kill him?"

James chose that moment to look at everything in the place but me.

"Lenny?"

"Stan . . . he wasn't a really nice man, you know?"

"I heard."

"So a lot of people probably wanted to kill him."

"Did he have a girl?" I watched him carefully again as I asked him this.

"No . . . no, Stan didn't have a girl."

"Nobody? Not even an ex-girlfriend?"

"Well . . . there might have been somebody, but she wasn't his girl, or anything."

"Then what?"

"I don't know. He just mentioned that he was . . . getting some from a pretty hot woman, but he never told me who she was."

"But she wasn't his girl?"

"He said she wasn't anybody's girl, that she was all for herself."

I wondered if he had been talking about Andrea Legend, or if there was a new player in the game.

I studied Lenny James as we talked, looking for signs that he might be gay. Nothing jumped out and waved at me.

"Lenny, because I'm working on Stan's case I want to ask you something. Don't get angry."

"Go ahead."

"Somebody told me they thought Stan might be . . . gay."

James made a disgusted sound.

"You been talkin' to his uncle, the old has-been. He sees gays in every corner."

"So Stan wasn't gay?"

"No . . . I am, but Stan wasn't. His uncle probably thought . . . but Stan never cared what his uncle thought."

"I thought Stan loved his uncle, wanted to be like him."

"Like Sammy Freed? Stan was better than that, Mr. Jacoby. Oh, maybe he saw his uncle on stage when he was a kid and that made him want to be a comic, but that was it. There was no way Stan wanted to be like his uncle."

"I'm going to ask you another personal question."

He looked sick but said, "Go ahead."

"If nobody liked Stan, why were you and he friends?"

"Who knows?" He shrugged his bony shoulders. "We just were. I can't explain it. He wasn't gay, and he was a lot smarter than me . . . I don't know."

"Was he helping you with your act?"

"Sometimes."

"Why would he help you and suspect everyone else of wanting to steal from him?"

"I told you, I don't know." He was becoming agitated, so I decided to let him go for now.

"Okay, Lenny. Thanks for taking the time to talk to me."

"Sure."

We both stood up. The waiter came over and I paid for the beer.

"Where do you live, Lenny?"

"I'm . . . stayin' with somebody right now. I don't have my own place."

"Well, if I wanted to ask you some more questions I guess I could find you here."

"Uh, yeah, sure."

"Thanks again."

I walked out of The Rodeo convinced that Lenny James was worried about more than being fired. He was too nervous to be telling the whole truth.

41

Now I HAD a problem. I wanted to check back at Packy's with Marty to see if he had found anything, but I also wanted to follow Lenny James. On the way out of the restaurant, I checked their hours and saw that they closed at eleven on weeknights, one A.M. on weekends. This was a Thursday.

I found a pay phone on the corner by the bookstore and called Packy's. Geneva answered.

"Is Marty back yet?"

"Not yet."

I looked at my watch and saw that it was a quarter after five. He might still be working at Waldrop's, or he could be on the way back. If he was going to be late back to Packy's, though, he would have called Geneva. If I called him at Waldrop's, would he answer the phone?

"Boss, you had a message."

"What message?"

"It was a man, and he said he was Ray Carbone."

"I'm listening."

"He wants you to meet him—wait, I've got it written down—at his place. You know the address?"

"I know it."

"He wants you there at midnight."

What was this all about? First he wanted me out of it, and now he wanted to meet me? Well, I knew he was going to continue to be hard to find. Maybe this would be the only way to do it.

"Is that it? No phone number?"

"No."

"Gen, did it sound like Ray?"

"I haven't talked to him often enough to know."

"Okay, thanks, Gen."

"When do you think Marty will be back? We're gettin' busy."

"I'm going to check right now."

"Boss?"

"Yeah?"

"You gonna keep this meetin'?"

"I've got to."

"Be careful, huh?"

"I'll see you before then."

I hung up and dialed Stan Waldrop's number. There was no answer. That was when I remembered that I had his answering machine tape. I hung up and looked around for a cab. I forgot about following Lenny James for the moment.

I went to put the key in the lock of Waldrop's apartment door, but there was no need. It was unlocked. I put the key away and wished I had a gun on me, but it was at home. I had practiced and practiced with the thing until I'd gotten pretty good at firing it, but I still didn't carry it around with me. The occasions when I wished I did were few and far between, but this was one of them.

I pushed the door open and went in slowly. On the off chance that Marty had gone out and left it unlocked when he returned, I called out to him.

"Marty!"

No answer.

He could have gone back to Packy's and left it unlocked.

Of course, there could have been someone else inside, and calling out would have alerted them, but it was too late to worry about that now.

The living room was a mess. There had either been a fight, or somebody had tossed it looking for something.

"Shit."

The kitchen was the same. As I passed it, I could see that the cabinets were open and the contents were all over the place.

I rushed to the bedroom, which was also a shambles. In the center of the mess was Marty, lying on his stomach. There was blood around his head on the rug.

"Fuck!" I shouted, and went to check him.

▽

42

"You finally hit the jackpot," Hocus said, "and I'm the prize."

We were in New York Hospital, on York Avenue in the sixties. He was referring to the fact that I'd finally found a body in his precinct.

Only it wasn't a body. Marty was still alive.

Once I discovered that Marty still had a pulse, I called an ambulance. They had the option of driving downtown to St. Vincent's, in the West Village, or across town to New York Hospital. I left the choice up to them. I just wanted to get him to the hospital.

From there I called Hocus and told him what had happened.

"I'll have a car go over there," he said. "You wait at the hospital for me."

When he arrived, I still had no word on Marty's condition.

"Okay, tell me what happened."

I gave it to him in a nutshell, even told him what I'd been doing while Marty was in Waldrop's apartment.

"I hope you had a key to that place."

"I did."

"What else does this have to do with?"

"Huh?"

"Which of the other bodies is this involved with?"

"Stan Waldrop, the stand-up comic who was killed in his dressing room the other night."

"Nothing to do with Ray's girlfriend?"

I shook my head.

"Different case."

"Okay, tell me about the comic."

I explained to Hocus why I'd been hired, and why I was continuing to work even though my client was dead.

"What was Marty looking for?"

"We didn't know. I just wanted him to get into the computer and look around."

"What happened to the computer?"

"It was on the floor when I got there. Probably got knocked over in a struggle."

"Where was Marty hit?"

"It looked like he was hit from behind, like Waldrop was."

"Then there couldn't have been a struggle, could there?"

"I guess not."

"That means whoever hit him meant to damage the computer so nobody could find what they were looking for."

"Yeah, but did *they* find what they were looking for?"

"What's Marty's condition?"

"I don't know yet. Why don't you flash your badge and go in and find out."

"Good idea. Wait here."

Instead of waiting right there I found a pay phone and called Geneva.

"Marty's not back yet, Boss, and I'm up to my pretty black ass in—"

"Marty's in the hospital, Gen."

"What? What happened?"

I explained about finding him and suggested she call Ed to cover.

"Either that or grab a regular and stick him behind the bar."

"Don't worry about it, I'll take care of it. You just take care of Marty."

"Okay."

"And let me know how he is?"

"I will."

I hung up and went back to the waiting room. Hocus appeared a few minutes later.

"How is he?"

"He needed a bunch of stitches to close a gash in the back of his head, and he has a concussion, but no fractures. He's gonna be okay."

"Jesus," I said, sitting down on the waiting-room sofa. My legs felt like noodles. "Thank God."

"I'm going over to the apartment, Jack. The doctors won't let me talk to him tonight. You might as well leave too. We can't see him until tomorrow."

I nodded.

"Feelin' guilty, huh?"

"Oh, yeah."

"Well, shake it off," he said. "Marty's a big boy, he could have said no when you asked him to help. Besides, who thought this would happen?"

"With one death already," I said, "why wouldn't it happen?"

43

I GOT BACK to Packy's at eleven and brought Geneva up to date on Marty. She hadn't been able to get Ed, so she had drafted Steve Stilwell to fill in behind the bar.

"Shots and beers, that's all I do," he said when I came in.

"Give me a beer. Icehouse."

Stilwell listened in while I told Geneva about Marty.

"Sounds like this joke case is gettin' serious," he said.

"There's more to it than jokes, Steve," I said. "There's got to be. Nobody kills for bad jokes."

"Bad jokes?"

I told him the fag joke Sam Freed had told me.

"What's that mean?" Geneva asked.

"I don't know, but if it's an example of Waldrop's jokes, who would want to steal them?"

"So what do you figure?" Stilwell asked.

"I don't know."

"What did Marty find?" Geneva asked.

"I don't know that, either. I can't talk to him until the morning."

"So what are you gonna do?" Geneva asked.

I looked at my watch. Ten after eleven. "I'm going to go over to Ray's apartment and see if he's there."

"Aren't you supposed to go at midnight?" Geneva asked.

"So I'll go early."

"You want some backup?" Stilwell asked.

"No," I said, "you stay here and back Geneva up."

"I feel so safe," she said, batting her eyelashes at him.

As I started for the door Stilwell yelled, "Hey, wait."

"What?"

"The apartment under Ray's?"

"Yeah?"

"As far as I can find out he wasn't being staked out by the cops."

"Vice?"

"No."

"What about the DEA?"

Stilwell frowned.

"You think Ray's involved in drugs?"

"No, I'm just asking questions. The FBI? Maybe the IRS?"

"If it's them I don't want to know about it," Stilwell said.

"Okay, so whoever the man and woman were, they weren't cops."

"Maybe they really were there just for a roll in the hay."

"Maybe, but I'm not ready to buy that yet. If I'm not back by closing, Gen, I'll see you tomorrow."

"I'm gonna go and see Marty in the morning."

"Then maybe I'll see you there."

"Be careful," she called out as I went out the door.

I grabbed a cab that had just let off a fare and gave the driver Ray's address. Keeping in mind what had happened to Joy, somebody else was looking for Ray. If this was some kind of setup, maybe I'd defeat it by arriving early.

44

I HAD THE cab drop me off down the block from Ray's building. During the ride I found myself wishing I had only one case to work on, but which one? I couldn't give up on Ray, he was my friend. Besides, I wanted to find out who killed Joy.

And then there was Stan Waldrop. He had paid me, and even though the money was almost used up, there was now Marty to consider. He was just lucky that he hadn't been hit on the head as hard as Waldrop had been, or he'd be dead too.

In the beginning I could have begged off either case, and now I couldn't give up either one.

I walked on the sidewalk across the street from Ray's building and watched it for a few minutes. There was a light on in a front first-floor apartment, and one on the third floor. Other than that the building was dark.

If the message I'd gotten was from Ray, then he'd be waiting for me inside. I'd know that when I rang the bell. However, if there was somebody else waiting for me in there, ringing the bell would let them know I was early.

I decided to use my old route.

I went around to the back of the building and went through the same ritual to retrieve the fire escape ladder. I was about to climb up it when somebody grabbed me from behind, and I knew I'd been had.

He yanked me down and hit me in the kidney. It was a good shot, expertly administered, and my body was suddenly paralyzed. The next thing I knew I was on the ground being kicked. The blows were not coming haphazardly. I was being worked over by somebody who knew what he was doing. Actually, the initial kidney shot helped a lot, because I couldn't even feel some of the ensuing blows.

Then one sharp blow must have struck a nerve or something because my leg shot out and made contact with an empty garbage can. It fell over noisily and started rolling. If you know what a rolling metal garbage can sounds like you can imagine the racket.

A back light went on and somebody hissed, "Shit!"

A mouth was near my ear and he whispered, "Forget about Danny Pesce, and stop looking for Ray Carbone. This is your only warning."

"What the hell is goin' on?" somebody shouted, and another light went on.

Footsteps began to recede and I was—it seemed like hours later—able to move a little. I hadn't realized I was curled into a fetal position until I straightened out.

The garbage can stopped rolling and whoever shouted had gotten no response, so the light went out and I was once again in darkness. Kicking over the can had saved me from a much worse beating, maybe even saved my life.

I tried to get to my feet, and now I could feel pain in several parts of my body, not the least of which was my right kidney area. I'd been hit in the kidneys plenty of times in the ring, and it was never a pretty sight when you took a leak later on. There was something disconcerting about pissing blood.

Somebody moaned and I realized it was me, but at least I was standing, although not very straight.

I looked up at the fire escape ladder. There was no way I was going to retrieve it again. My body just wasn't up to the job. Besides, it was pretty obvious now that Ray wasn't going to be up there waiting for me. I'd been set up by somebody who knew I had used the fire escape before. Who knew that? I hadn't told anyone. The only people who could have known were the man and the woman in the fourth-floor apartment.

They must have heard me coming up the fire escape and jumped in bed together to fool me into thinking they were just a randy couple.

Maybe cops weren't staking Ray out, but somebody had been, probably the same person who had just given me an expert going-over.

It didn't escape my attention as I staggered back to the street that one man I knew who was capable of that kind of expert work was Mr. Ray Carbone himself.

45

"Here," Geneva said, handing me a bunch of ice cubes wrapped in a towel, "you got kicked in the head at least once."

"That kidney shot kept me from knowing it until now."

I took the ice and held it to the swelling on my forehead.

"Do you think it was Ray?" Stilwell asked.

I must have been in that alley longer than I thought, because by the time I got back to Packy's, Stilwell had been helping Geneva close up. Now they were both in the kitchen with me, and Geneva wanted me to go to the hospital.

"I've been beat up plenty of times, Gen. I'd know if I was seriously hurt."

"Suit yourself."

I looked at Stilwell and said, "I don't think Ray would have done this to me. Besides, it didn't sound like his voice."

"You said he was whispering. A whisper can disguise a voice, and I'd bet Ray Carbone has experience with administering a beating like this one."

"I'm sure he's done it once or twice, but I don't think he did it to me tonight. In fact, it's pretty obvious the message wasn't from Ray. I should have realized it before."

"How?"

"Which phone did the call come in on, Gen?"

"The bar phone."

I looked at Stilwell.

"Ray would have called my office phone. I should have known that."

"Hey," Stilwell said, "you walked in with your eyes open. You even assumed it was some kind of trap and went to use the fire escape."

"And he was waiting for me. He out-thought me."

"You're working on two cases," Geneva said. "He's only working on you."

"Nice try, but I still feel like a putz."

"A putz?" Geneva said. "Putz. I have to remember that."

"Go home, Gen," I said. "I'm all right."

She looked at Stilwell and he nodded and said, "'Night, Gen. Thanks for letting me behind the bar."

"I only let you behind there because I knew I was safe."

"Because I'm a cop?"

"No," she said, "because everybody knows that you and that big partner of yours are gay."

She left and Stilwell looked at me. "Is she kidding?"

"Yes."

He hesitated a moment, then said, "I knew that."

I took the ice off my head and put it down.

"How's your head?"

"It hurts."

"You should have it checked."

"If it still hurts in the morning, I'll be at the hospital to see Marty. I can have it checked then."

"Wait a minute."

He took a small pencil flashlight from his pocket.

"Sometimes I forget I have this. Look straight ahead."

I did as he said and he directed the pencil flash into my left eye, then my right, then again and again.

"Pupils are reacting," he said, putting the flash away. "You don't have a concussion."

"Thanks, Steve."

"You want me to help you get home?"

"No, I'm going to stay here tonight. I've got a cot in the office."

"You think whoever kicked the shit out of you knows where you live?"

"No, I'm just too tired to leave. You go ahead. I'll see you tomorrow, maybe."

"Maybe," he said. "Bruce and I have some things to do tomorrow."

"How's your case coming?"

"Slowly," he said. "I think IAD is letting us twist in the wind because they think we'll get nervous."

"Are you nervous?"

"We don't have any reason to be nervous," he said. "We're innocent."

As he left I wondered how many men he'd heard that from in his career as a policeman.

46

I WOKE UP the next morning confused and disoriented. I lay there for a few scary moments, wondering where I was. As I tried to sit up, my entire body protested and brought back the events of the night before.

I sat on the cot, staring down between my feet. I knew where I was and what had happened, but I couldn't seem to make up my mind about my next move. It was frightening. I started to wonder if Stilwell had been wrong and I did have a concussion. The one time I had walked out of the ring concussed I had blacked out and couldn't remember an entire three-day period.

I checked my watch, not for the time, but for the date. I was relieved to see I hadn't misplaced a day anywhere.

I keep fresh clothes in the office, and there's a shower in the back bathroom. I stood under the hot spray, and when I came out I felt a lot better. There had been a hazy edge to everything when I first woke up, but the shower seemed to have dispelled that. Also, the heat had taken some of the ache out of my bruises and my joints. I got dressed and checked my watch again. It was almost ten, an hour past visiting hours at the hospital.

I sat at my desk for a moment and made sure I had everything I wanted to carry with me. Once again I had Geneva's little recorder and the answering machine message tapes in my pockets. I realized I had not yet gotten a chance to listen to Stan Waldrop's tape. I was going to make sure I heard it before the day was out.

Besides the .38 at my apartment, I also kept a little .25 caliber Beretta in my desk at the office, just in case of trouble. I had an ankle holster for it, and before leaving I strapped it on, checked the gun to be sure it was loaded and working, slid it into the holster, and then left the store. Too many people were dying or getting hurt, and the next time something happened I was going to be armed and ready.

Outside I hailed a cab and told the cabbie to take me to New York Hospital.

When I got there, Geneva was in the waiting room, and told me there was a detective in with Marty. I described Hocus and she confirmed that it was him.

"I'll introduce you when he comes out."

"You don't have to," she said. "I've already met too many cops, knowing you. I just want to get in to see Marty, and then I've got to go and work out."

She was wearing her usual oversized sweatshirt over her workout clothes.

▽

47

"Marty," I said when I saw him sitting up in bed with his head all bandaged, "I'm really sorry."

"Forget it, Boss," he said. "Time and a half will cure anything, you know?"

"You got it."

"Great. What happened to your head?"

"I took a bit of a bump last night, too, but I'll tell you about it another time. For now, tell me what you found, if anything, before the ceiling fell in."

"I didn't find much of anything. I got into a couple of files. One was letters, another was like a phone book, but on a computer, you know?"

"That's all?"

"Well, there was another file, but I couldn't get into it without a password."

"Shit. Hocus says that the computer is smashed and the memory is gone. Now we'll never know what was in that file."

"Not necessarily."

"What do you mean? Is there something you didn't tell Hocus? You're not supposed to hold out on the cops, you know, Marty."

He shrugged and said, "I didn't know if you'd want me to give it to the cops or to you."

"Give me what?"

"This."

He reached under his pillow and took out a small blue square of plastic with a piece of flat metal on it.

"What's that?"

"A floppy disk."

I took it from him and found it pretty solid.

"It doesn't feel floppy."

"Well, the first disks were five and a quarter inches square, and they were, uh, well, floppy. Now these disks are three and a half inches, and more solid, but they still call them floppy disks."

"And what is on this particular floppy disk?"

He smiled.

"Everything that was on the hard drive."

"Meaning what?" I asked, and then added, "and go slow for me, Marty."

"Even though the computer's memory was wiped out, I've got everything on here."

"It all fits on here?"

"There wasn't that much on the drive, Boss. Apparently he didn't use the computer much, or he just got it."

"So what do I have to do?"

"Just get access to somebody's computer and print out what's on that disk."

"And the file with the password?"

He shrugged. "I can't help you there. You've got to figure out the password before you can print the file."

"Okay. Do you know somebody whose computer I can use?"

"I'd let you use mine, but I'm stuck here for a while."

"So who do you know?"

"Are they gonna get hit on the head?"

"The truth? I don't know."

"Let me make a few calls."

"I'll try to keep it from happening."

"Why not take it to the cops? They have computers."

"They might print it all out and not let me have a look. You went to all the trouble to give this to me instead of them, I'd like to see what's on it before I give it up."

"Okay, so I'll make a few calls and get back to you."

"All right. Maybe I can think of someone in the meantime."

"Those flowers for me?"

"Oh, yeah," I said, handing them to him. "From Gen."

"Is she outside?"

"She had to go work out."

"Oh."

"Have a nurse put them in some water."

"Sure."

Suddenly he looked like his eyelids were getting heavy.

"Let me get out of here and let you get some rest. Marty, I'm really sorry—"

"Forget it, Boss," he said, yawning. "I'll be back to work in no time."

"Just make sure you're well enough first."

"Am I gettin' time and a half while I'm in here?" he called out as I walked to the door.

I turned and said, "Don't push it."

48

WHEN I LEFT the hospital the floppy disk was in my pocket along with the message tapes and the small recorder. I was really starting to feel like I had one foot in the past. Maybe a few courses in electronics would help.

I grabbed a cab back to my apartment, stopping across the street at the sandwich deli for a ham and egg on a roll and two containers of black coffee. I ate the sandwich seated at my kitchen table with the recorder, tapes, and disk lined up in front of me. What I needed was somebody with their own equipment, somebody whose safety I wouldn't be endangering by involving them. The answer, when it came, was so clear it amazed me.

My new partner, Walker Blue.

After eating, I went to Packy's and found Geneva behind the bar. Aside from her, the place was empty.

"How's Marty?" she asked.

"He's fine. I gave him your flowers."

"Good."

"Ed coming in today?"

"I called him last night and he agreed to work a double shift."

"You won't have to put Stilwell behind the bar again."

"That's good," she said, "he doesn't know a highball from a baseball."

"He's a cop," I said in his defense. "All they know is beer."

Okay, it was sort of a defense.

I went into the office and pulled Walker's partnership papers out of the drawer. I went through them, hoping I'd be able to understand it all without a lawyer. It wasn't that I thought Walker would try to pull anything, I just wanted to know what I was signing before I signed it.

After I went through the papers, I realized I might have to ask Heck to look through them for me—and then it hit me. Heck had to have computer equipment in his office, and Missy was the one who would operate it. That would save me from having to ask Walker to help even before we were officially partners.

Since that appealed to me more, I put the papers back in the envelope, then put the disk in there with them. As an afterthought I added the message tapes and closed the whole thing up with the metal clasp.

"I'll probably be out most of the day," I said to Geneva on my way out.

"What else is new?"

I waved and went out the door.

"Heck's in court, Miles," Missy said as I entered.

"Why do you assume I'm here to see him?" I asked. "What if I was here to see you?"

She started to smile, then frowned.

"What happened to your face?"

"It looks worse than it is."

In addition to the bruise on my forehead, it turned out that I had one or two others on my face as well. I looked a little bit like I did after my last fight.

I approached Missy's desk, but instead of looking at her I was looking at her computer.

"What can I do for you, Miles?"

"I need a favor."

"So much for wanting to talk to me. When's the last time we had lunch?"

"Uh, last week."

"Two months ago."

"We'll have lunch next week."

"Sure, I've heard that before. You know, for the one-millionth time, I'm glad we're just friends. If we were going out together you'd drive me nuts."

"Luckily," I said, "that's never been a problem."

We both liked it that way.

"What do you need?"

"I've got a computer disk here, a floppy disk."

"Let's see it."

I took it out and showed it to her.

"Will this fit your machine?"

"I have a hard drive, a five and a quarter and a three and a half on my machine."

A couple of days ago she would have lost me right before "hard drive."

I looked at her computer and saw the name IBM on it. Nothing but top of the line for Heck.

"I need to know what's on that disk, Missy."

"You need hard copies?"

"Yes." I felt smug about not having to ask what a "hard copy" was.

"Doesn't Walker Blue have his own equipment?"

"We haven't signed partnership papers yet. That's my other favor."

I put the envelope down on her desk.

"I wonder if Heck would have time to look them over before I sign them?"

"I can ask," she said, "or I can look at them. After all, I type all of Heck's contracts. There's not much I don't know about them."

"Hey, that'd be great, Missy."

"I'll look them over while I'm printing out this disk. You want everything on it?"

"Yep. Oh, wait, there's a file on there that needs a password."

"Do you know it?"

"No," I said, "but I'm going to try to find out or figure it out. Just do everything else and I'll get back to you."

"Okay."

"I really appreciate this, Missy."

"You'll pay."

"I will?"

She nodded.

"Once you start working with Walker, I'll be able to stick you for a real expensive lunch."

"You got it. The sky's the limit."

"You'll be sorry you said that."

"Do you know what's happening with Danny Pesce?"

"Heck's working on getting a reduced charge so Mr. Pesce can get bail. He's not very hopeful, though. The DA is being very tough on this one. I think he thinks he's got a big fish on the hook."

I have her a look and asked, "Was that a pun, Missy?"

She stared at me blankly for a moment, then smiled and said, "I guess it was, wasn't it?"

$\triangledown$

49

I THOUGHT ABOUT using Missy's phone before I left, but since I was going to ask somebody to lunch I thought it advisable to use a pay phone outside.

When I dialed Jonathan Healy's office, Andrea answered, as I'd hoped.

"Have you had lunch yet?"

There was a long pause and then she said, "Miles?"

"Oh, good. I thought you were going to deal my ego a huge blow there."

"What—"

"I asked if you'd had lunch, yet."

"Uh, no, but—"

"How about half an hour. I'll come up there, and you pick the place."

"I thought—after what happened—"

"At your apartment? That was a little tiff. Besides, this is business. I want to talk about Stan Waldrop."

"I-I'll have to get back in an hour or so. I have a conference call."

"No problem."

"Why don't you meet me somewhere? It will save time."

"Name it."

She thought a moment and then asked, "How about Ellen's Stardust Diner?"

"That sounds good." Ellen's was on the corner of Fifty-sixth and Sixth, an honest-to-God diner with home cooking and, on certain nights, singing waiters. It was famous for having turned Axl Rose of Guns 'n' Roses away when he asked for a table for six for him and his girlfriend.

"Half an hour," I said, and we hung up.

When I got to Ellen's, Andrea was already seated at a table along the left wall. Placed strategically and high up were television picture tubes showing fifties TV shows and commercials, and movies.

Andrea looked very smart in a red blazer with a ruffly white blouse underneath. She had a glass of iced tea on the table in front of her.

"Sorry I'm late."

I had taken the subway instead of a cab and had gotten stuck in a tunnel.

"Just a few minutes," she said. "It's all right. Can we order quickly, though? I do have to get back."

We called a very personable young waiter over and while she ordered meat loaf, I simply ordered a hamburger because I thought there was a good chance I wasn't going to get to eat lunch once we started talking.

"This is the only place in the city I'll order meat loaf," she said. "You never know what some places put in it."

"And here you do know?"

"No, but it's so good I don't care."

I also ordered an iced tea.

"What did you want to know about Stan?" she asked.

"I want to know everything about Stan. Mostly I want to know why he came to me to find some jokes that had been stolen when there's obviously something else going on."

"What makes you say that?"

"Number one, he's dead. Right there's a good indication. Number two, your little seduction scene."

"I thought—"

"And number three, a friend of mine was attacked yesterday in Stan's apartment which, by the way, was torn apart by someone who was looking for something."

She hesitated a moment, then asked, "Did they find anything?"

"I don't think so. The apartment was gone through completely. Unless they found what they were looking for in the very last place they looked, I don't think they found it at all. Oh, by the way, they smashed Stan's computer."

"Why would they do that?"

"I don't know."

"Do you think what they were looking for was in the computer?"

"I want you to tell me what they were looking for, Andrea."

"How would I know?"

"Why were you going to try to seduce me the other night?"

"I wasn't!"

"You know," I said, "I should have let you go through with it. It might have been fun."

She gave me a haughty look, raising one eyebrow, and said, "You'll never know."

"No, I probably won't, but I will find out what you're hiding, Andrea."

"I'm not hiding anything."

"What was Stan doing in Vegas?"

"Why are you interested in that?"

"Because it wasn't until he came back from Vegas that he noticed his jokes were missing from his computer. Everything seems to have happened since Vegas."

"He was performing, that's all."

"Maybe I should go to Vegas and ask some questions."

"That would be up to you."

Lunch came, but she ignored her plate. I took a bite of my excellent burger.

"What are you thinking?" I asked.

"I'm wondering why I agreed to come here."

"You know, I was wondering the same thing. You know what I think?"

"What?"

"I think you want to talk to me. I think maybe you're in over your head and you can use my help."

"In what?"

"That's what I want to know."

"I think you're grabbing at straws, Miles. Isn't that money that Stan paid you almost used up? The police are working on his murder. Why aren't they bothering me the way you are?"

"I don't know," I said. "Maybe I should have a talk with them. As for the money Stan paid me, I think I'll just donate the remainder of my services to his memory."

She grabbed her purse and said, "I have to be going."

"What about your meat loaf?"

"You're paying," she said, getting up. "You eat it."

I watched her leave, then looked down at my burger. I finished it, and then slid her plate over to me. After one bite of the meat loaf I knew I'd finish it. She was right. Who cared what they put in it if it tasted this good?

Andrea had brought up a good point, and that was about the cops. Maybe it was time for me to talk to the detectives again and see just where they were on Stan's murder.

After the meat loaf, of course.

▽

50

I CALLED THE Sixth Precinct to see if Detective Pell was in, and he was. He agreed to see me if I came right over.

When I got there he was seated behind his desk, looking well groomed and unruffled. The other detectives in the room—three of them, including his partner, Matthews— were all in shirt sleeves and looking harried.

"How do you stay so cool?" I asked.

He looked up at me and said, "It's hereditary. Have a seat."

I sat opposite him and he gave me his immediate attention. I was not used to dealing with cops like him. Even Hocus, who I considered my friend, hardly ever gave me his undivided attention.

"What happened to your face?"

"I walked into a door."

He shook his head slightly. "What have you got for me?"

I sat there for a minute, confused as to which case he was handling, Joy's murder or Stan Waldrop's. When I finally figured it out, I told him what had happened to Marty in Waldrop's apartment yesterday.

"So you think this has something to do with his murder?"

"Don't you?"

"It's possible."

"Have you keyed in on any suspects yet?"

"Not many."

"No?"

He frowned. "Why does that surprise you?"

"Well, I've talked to a few people—uh, in the course of

looking for the missing jokes, of course—and I've found out that he wasn't very well liked."

"Who have you talked to?"

"His uncle, and a man who claims to have been his friend."

"We talked to the uncle. My partner remembers having seen him in the Catskills when he was a kid."

"That must have gone a long way with him."

Pell permitted himself a small smile and said, "It did."

"What about Lenny James? Did you talk to him?"

He nodded. "The uncle told us about him. Told us he was his nephew's gay lover. He also suggested that his nephew might have been involved in some illegal activities."

"Like what?"

Pell shrugged.

"Drugs?"

"He didn't say."

"Is Lenny James a suspect?"

"Everybody's a suspect, Jacoby. Everybody who knew him. You know that."

"Except me, right?"

Pell remained silent.

"Have you looked into Vegas?"

Pell frowned again. I had the feeling that when he was fifty he'd still look like a big little boy.

"What about Vegas?"

"Waldrop was in Vegas last week, performing."

"So?"

"I just thought maybe something might have happened while he was there."

"Where was he performing?"

"The Aladdin."

He picked up a pencil, scribbled something, and put it down quickly. "I'll look into it."

"What about this agent?"

"Jonathan Healy?"

"Andrea Legend. She works for Healy, handling clients on

her own. Waldrop was one of them."

"Nice kind of agent to have."

"Was he involved with her, personally?"

"She says no."

"Well, of course she says no."

"I've seen some photos of him, Jacoby," he said. "What would he be doing with her?"

"Maybe the question should be, what would she be doing with him?"

"We haven't found any evidence that there was anything sexual going on."

"What about this Allegretto guy?"

"How do you mean?"

"Was he involved with Andrea?"

"What's that got to do with anything?"

"Well, maybe she had him kill Stan."

"He was out front with you when Waldrop was killed."

"What if he killed Stan and then came out front?"

"What if you did that?"

"Hey, I'm trying to help here."

"Maybe you're just trying to get suspicion off yourself."

"Get real, Pell."

"Do you have something solid to offer me on this investigation, Mr. Jacoby?"

"I just thought—"

"Because if you don't, I'll have to ask you to leave. I have a lot of work to do."

I stared at him for a moment, but I'd suddenly lost his attention. He was now treating me like every other cop did.

All was right with the world again, right?

I got up and started to leave, but just as I was going out, Detective Sandoval was coming in with his partner, Yearwood, right behind him.

"Look who's here," Yearwood said.

"Looking for us, Jacoby?" Sandoval asked.

"As a matter of fact, no. I was just talking to Detective Pell."

"Ah," Sandoval said, "the detective on the other murder you're involved in. And now I hear you almost had another? A friend of yours?"

"You talked to Detective Hocus, I take it."

"Oh, yes," Sandoval said, "he wanted to coordinate with us. I think we finally decided that if you left New York for good, there'd be less work for us."

"I think we could even get young Pell there to agree." Yearwood threw in her two cents.

"You guys are funny."

"Really? Maybe you could get us an agent?"

"Sorry," I said, moving past them, "but I'm on the outs with the only agent I know."

"What happened to your face, Jacoby?" Yearwood asked.

"I bruised myself shaving."

I left, thinking that I just didn't have the knack for this comedy thing.

▽

51

I WANTED TO talk to Sammy Freed again. He hadn't mentioned anything to me about illegal activities. Why would he say something like that to the police?

Rather than deli hop to find out where he was today, I went to his building. The same doorman was on duty, and we went through the same routine.

"For an extra ten," he said, after I had given him twenty, "I can give you his schedule."

"What schedule?"

"Monday he goes to the New York Deli, Tuesday, Wolf's, and so on."

"This is Thursday."

He waited to see if I was going to give him an extra ten, and when I didn't he shrugged and said, "The Stage."

The Stage Deli is on Seventh Avenue between Fifty-third and Fifty-fourth streets. The front is all glass, and I could see Sammy Freed sitting in a corner, right by the window. At the moment, there were two waitresses listening to him as he spoke. As I entered, the two women—both in their late forties or early fifties—broke into laughter and walked away from him, shaking their heads. There were two other waitresses working, and they were considerably younger. They were shaking their heads in a different way. I was willing to bet they had never even heard of the Catskills.

One of them started toward me and I said, "I'm meeting Sammy."

"Sorry to hear it," she said, and turned around.

I walked over to where Freed was sitting, now looking out the window.

"Hi, Sammy."

He looked up quickly, frowned as he spotted me, and then smiled. His rug was on straighter today.

"Honest Jack, the detective," he said. "Sit down, sit down."

Since it was way past lunchtime, all he had in front of him was a cup of coffee. I wondered how long he stayed at these delis every day.

"You come to talk some more to an old man?"

"I came to find out why an old man told the cops his nephew was involved in something illegal."

He stared at me, and just for a moment I thought I saw Sammy Freed, King of the Catskills, fall away, replaced by Sam Friedlander. Who was Sam Friedlander, I wondered, before he became Sammy Freed?

He looked out the window, and when he looked back Sammy Freed was in place.

"What's going on, Sam?"

"Hey, what do I know? I'm a dumb old Jew, but that kid, he was up to something."

"Why do you say that?"

"Because he was antsy, that's why. Something had him pretty nervous—and I'll tell you another thing. Whatever he was into, that *fagele* boyfriend was in it, too."

"Sammy, you don't know for sure your nephew was gay, do you?"

"I know that James kid was, and why would Stan be friends with him otherwise?"

I was fighting some deep-rooted old prejudices here. In Sam Friedlander's book, only someone who is gay would be friends with someone who is gay.

"Sam, what do you think it was, drugs?"

"I don't know what it was," he said, violently waving away the question. "You think I want to know?"

"Then why tell the cops?"

"Because they're trying to find out who killed him. I shouldn't tell them what I think? What I suspect?"

"Why didn't you tell me?"

"Because you're looking for his meshuganah jokes, not his killer. Why should I tell you?"

He had a point there. Still, I thought the old Jewish comic act was not quite as real as it had been the first time. He was still, however, coming off as a lonely old man who spent his time in delis just to be around people. How much of what he told the cops was just because he wanted someone to talk to?

"Would you tell me now, Sam? If I asked you?"

"I don't know, kid, I really don't," he said. "If I did, I woulda tried to talk him out of it."

"So you think whatever he was into got him killed?"

"What else? Bad jokes? If that killed people, anybody who ever listened to Berle would be dead."

"Okay, Sam," I said. "Okay."

I couldn't remember if I'd left him a card yesterday, so I took one out and handed it to him.

"If you do think of something, let me know, huh? Just because I'm looking for his jokes doesn't mean I won't stumble across his killer."

"Sure, sure," he said, putting the card down on the table. "I'll call."

I left the Stage Deli and walked past him as he was staring out the window. The look on his face was yet another I hadn't seen before. Maybe he was thinking about the old days in the Catskills. Or maybe about Stanley Waldropsky when he was a small boy. Or maybe he was just staring across the street at Lindy's, trying to decide if he wanted to go in there for cheesecake.

It sounded good to me, so I went across and had some.

52

WHEN I CAME out, Freed was still sitting in the window of the Stage. I went over to the Sheraton, where it would be easier to grab a cab, and took one back to Packy's.

Much of what I do takes place in my head. I learned a little about that from Eddie Waters, but a lot more about it during the past few years. I'm a much better detective today than I was when I first started out, and I'm still learning. Going into partnership with Walker Blue and working with him would be a real learning experience. Maybe I'd find out some other way to do it, but right now I needed very much to turn things over and over in my head, ask question after question of myself until something popped into place. That was what I did in the cab.

Could it be that Waldrop really was involved in something illegal, but got upset enough about his jokes being stolen that he hired me anyway? Didn't he realize that in the course of my investigation I might turn up something on his other activities? Or were his jokes ever really stolen? If not, why use that as an excuse to hire me? What was it he really wanted me to do?

Or was Sammy Freed way off the mark? Maybe Waldrop really was just after his jokes, but in light of his murder and the attack on Marty, that didn't seem feasible. Even Andrea Legend's attitude indicated that something else was going on.

In order to find out for sure, who was there to ask? Andrea? If she knew anything, I was sure it wouldn't be the whole story.

Lenny James? I didn't think he would offer anything if he was in on it—especially if Waldrop was killed because of it. James would be scared shitless.

On the other hand, if James and Waldrop were involved in something illegal, and it had gotten Waldrop killed, why wouldn't James leave town? Unless he killed Waldrop. Was it James who attacked Marty while he was looking for something in Waldrop's apartment?

And why kill Stan Waldrop if he was the only one who knew where the elusive "it" was?

This was starting to sound a little like a case Nick Delvecchio had worked on a few years back, when he and some other people were looking for something they called "The Hole Thing." As it turned out, Nick never did find out what was in the "thing."

Now I had some people looking for "it," and at least one man had died because of "it," and Marty had been attacked because of "it."

I didn't think I'd be satisfied if this ended the way Delvecchio's case had.

I wanted to know what "it" was.

When I got to Packy's the place was busy. We didn't do dinner, but we did a strong after-dinner crowd, and they were starting to trickle in. Ed was behind the bar, and Geneva was working the floor.

I waved at both of them and went on into the office. I took Geneva's recorder from my pocket and laid it on the desk. I went into my other pocket, and that's when I remembered that the message tapes had been in the envelope with the partnership papers I'd left with Missy. I called Missy but there was no answer. Apparently the Heck Delgado office was closed for the day. I called her home number, but there was no answer there, either.

The red light on my machine was winking at me, so I hung up and pressed the "play" button.

"Miles, it's Walker Blue. I just wanted to be sure you

received the partnership papers. Have someone check them over for you and then sign them and get them back to me as soon as possible. I am anxious to get this partnership going."

I was flattered. I was anxious to get it going, too, but I had two things I had to clear up before I could.

I had turned the Stan Waldrop case over and over in my mind in the cab, and the thing that was eating at me was Vegas. Something was bothering me, and I thought it was the fact that Stan Waldrop did not strike me as the kind of talent who would play Vegas. If that was true, what was he doing there? I wondered idly what Lenny James, Andrea Legend, and Sammy Freed were doing that week.

Now I sat back in my chair and started putting the other case through the same paces.

Danny Pesce had been arrested for killing Michael Bonetti, a bookie. For some reason, Pesce wanted Ray Carbone brought in as his witness, but Carbone was on the run. I knew Ray, and I knew he wouldn't be running if he was just a witness. Somehow, he was more involved in the killing than that. The evidence of that was that someone was looking for him bad enough to torture Joy to find out if she knew where he was, and then kill her.

Had she known?

Had she given him up?

Was he lying dead somewhere as a result?

Why hadn't he called me for help, rather than calling me to warn me off? He'd helped me often enough to know that I owed him.

That was what really puzzled me. What was going on that Ray didn't want me to have any part of?

Who to ask? Truman Tyler? Did he know more than he was saying? Danny Pesce certainly knew more, but he was too busy being a stand-up guy, like he'd been taught growing up. My God, even in grammar school kids learned not to rat on other kids.

Wait a minute.

Heck.

Heck Delgado was Danny Pesce's lawyer. Whatever Pesce told Heck was privileged information. Could it be that Pesce had told Heck more than Heck was telling me? Why would Heck keep it in, though, if it would help me find Ray? Why risk his client? Over ethics?

Knowing Heck Delgado, that was exactly what he would do.

I was at a dead end with Ray unless Nick Delvecchio turned up something on Truman Tyler that I could use, or Heck knew more than he was saying and I could get him to tell me.

Or unless Ray decided on his own that he wanted me to find him.

None of those things seemed likely to happen tonight, though, and I felt as if I hadn't slept in my own bed for a month.

I left the recorder in the desk and went out to the bar.

"I'm going home to bed," I said to Geneva. "If anyone calls, tell them I died."

"That's not funny."

I turned and looked at her and said, "Yeah, you're right. I'm tired, Gen. I'm going home."

"See you tomorrow, Boss."

I waved and went out to get a cab to take me home to bed.

53

I WOKE IN the morning with two thoughts.

One, I had to go to Las Vegas.

Two, I had to have a frank talk with Heck Delgado.

I was going to have to put both of them off for the moment, though, because when I got up and walked into my kitchen I had company.

"Hello, Ray."

Carbone looked at me from one of my kitchen chairs.

"You're a sound sleeper, Jack."

"I've been keeping late hours."

"Working hard?"

"Oh, yeah."

"Looking for me." It was a statement.

"For one."

"Working more than one case?"

"Uh-huh. You want some coffee?"

"Sure."

"You want to put that gun away?"

He looked down at the gun he was holding in his lap as if he'd forgotten it was there.

"You don't need it, you know."

It was an automatic. It was a Hechler & Koch. I wasn't sure of the caliber, but I was sure that it carried eighteen shots. Ray was wishy-washy on the caliber of guns he used, but he insisted on having enough shots to do the job.

He lifted the gun and tucked it away inside his jacket, probably in a shoulder holster.

"Sorry," he said.

I went to the counter to load the coffeemaker. I was wearing a T-shirt and jockey shorts, but if Ray didn't mind, I didn't, either.

"I thought I asked you to stop looking for me. Didn't you get my message?"

"You left me a message on your own machine."

"When I heard your voice, I knew you'd taken my tape. Anything interesting on it?"

"A couple of messages from Truman Tyler, a couple from Joy."

"Joy's dead."

"I wondered if you knew."

"I know."

When the coffeemaker was going, I turned to face him.

"What's going on, Ray?"

"You look beat up."

"I got ambushed in back of your building."

"How'd you manage that?"

"Somebody called the bar and said they were you, wanted me to meet you at your place."

"I didn't call."

"I know that . . . now."

"Sorry. I was trying to keep you out of it, you know."

"I'm in it, Ray. I'm supposed to be working for Heck Delgado, and he's working for Danny Pesce."

"He thinks he's working for Danny Pesce."

"What do you mean?"

"It's complicated."

"I've got time."

He stood up. "I don't."

"Aren't you going to have some coffee?"

"I changed my mind."

He started for the door, then held his hand out when I started away from the counter.

"Don't, Jack."

"You look beat, Ray. Have you eaten?"

"Not much."

I went to the refrigerator and took out half a deli sandwich I had wrapped in aluminum foil a few days earlier. It was probably still good. I tossed it to him.

"Thanks."

"Wait a few minutes," I said, "I'll give you a thermos of coffee."

He weighed my offer and then nodded shortly.

"Why are you on the run, Ray?"

"Bonetti was connected, Jack. He was Family."

"So?"

"So I killed him."

I hesitated, then said, "Run that by me again, will you?"

"I killed him."

"You beat him to death, Ray?"

"I beat on him," Ray said. "He fell, he hit his head. I was bodyguarding Pesce; Bonetti and two others came at him."

"Two others?"

"They weren't good men. See, Bonetti was working independent, and the boys didn't know about it. He had his own boys, but they were cheap muscle. I took care of them and then started in on him."

"Did you kill them?"

"No, I just put them out of commission."

"What was Pesce doing?"

"Watching."

"He hasn't given you up."

Ray shrugged.

"He's a stand-up guy."

"Yeah."

"What about Truman Tyler?"

"He knew Bonetti was working on his own. He was working with him."

"Why? Why would Bonetti go against the Family?"

"Because he was connected, but he was cheap. He was

actually somebody's cousin once or twice removed, you know? He wasn't going to move up the ladder very much, so he decided to make some money on his own."

"Why don't you tell somebody?"

"Tell who? Who's gonna listen to an ex-pug works as a bodyguard?"

"I will."

He laughed shortly.

"Another ex-pug who works keyholes. You and me, we won't carry much weight with the boys, Jack."

He might have been right about that.

"Coffee's ready."

I leaned down and took a thermos bottle from a cabinet. I emptied the pot into it and closed it tight.

"Here."

I handed it across to him.

"Put it on the table."

"You think I'm going to try something, Ray?"

"You're my friend, Jack, I know that. You'd try something and think you're doing me a favor, but you wouldn't be. Put it on the table."

I did as he said, and backed away. He picked it up and held it in both hands.

"What about Pesce? You going to let him go up for what you did?"

"He'll talk eventually."

"He still might take the fall."

"I got to take that chance."

"Where are you going to go?"

"Away. Time for me to leave New York."

"This is your home, Ray."

"I'll get another home."

"They'll find you."

"If they keep looking, maybe. Maybe not."

"So that's it? Why not go to the cops? They'd keep you alive."

"What do you want me to do, Jack, go away on a manslaughter rap? How long would I last in the joint, a tasty morsel like me?"

He was kidding about the morsel part, but he was right. Somebody would put a shiv into him sooner or later, for one reason or another—maybe even for the boys.

"Too bad you've got to give up your life for a cheap bookie, Ray."

"A cheap, connected bookie."

"Do you have any money?"

"Some."

"Wait."

I went into the bedroom where I had a stash of bills in a big beer stein. I took it all out, carried it into the other room, and gave it to him without counting it.

"I don't know how much is there."

He put it in his pocket and said, "I appreciate it, Jack."

"Keep in touch, huh? Maybe something will come up."

"If they come after you, Jack, tell them you saw me and I left town."

"It's the truth," I said with a shrug. "What else would I tell them?"

"Yeah," he said. He held up the thermos and said, "Thanks for the coffee."

"I'm sorry about Joy, Ray."

He shrugged.

"That's my fault. I got to live with it. She didn't know where I was, she couldn't have told them anything."

"You're just going to let them get away with killing her?"

"Don't try that on me, Jack. Joy was okay, but she wasn't the great love of my life or anything. She's dead and I can't bring her back. Look, I gotta go."

"Good luck, Ray."

"Don't try to follow me."

"Not in my underwear."

He nodded, backed toward the door, and then went out.

Was that it, I wondered? Case solved? I tell Heck, he makes a deal for Danny Pesce? Joy White's killers go unpunished because they're connected?

This didn't leave much to talk frankly about with Heck.

I guessed I was going to Vegas.

▽

54

ACTUALLY, THERE WAS no way I could avoid telling Heck Delgado what had happened. I called the office early, got Missy, who told me that Heck would be there until ten. I got off the elevator at nine-thirty.

"He's inside,"she said as I came in. "Do you want that computer stuff?"

"After I come out, Missy. I want to talk to him before he has to leave."

"Okay."

I went into Heck's office, and he looked up from his desk and waved.

"I've got half an hour."

"This shouldn't take that long. I had a visitor this morning."

"Oh? Who?" He was looking at a piece of paper, or a file, on his desk.

"Ray Carbone."

That brought his head up quickly.

"You found him?"

"He found me. I woke up to find him in my kitchen."

"Where is he now?"

"Gone."

"Gone? Gone where?"

"I don't know. He said he was leaving town."

He sat back in his chair and gave me all of his attention.

"I have got to hear this."

I gave him my conversation with Ray almost verbatim. He listened calmly and quietly until I was done.

"Will you testify?" he asked when I finished.

"About what?"

"About what he told you?"

"I will, but it would be hearsay."

He waved that away.

"I know, but I'd want a jury to hear it anyway."

"Well . . . sure."

"Fine."

"That's it?"

"What else is there?" he asked. "You've told me he's gone, and that he confessed."

"To manslaughter, not murder."

"That doesn't matter to me. I know he's your friend, Miles, but I'm concerned with my client, not with him."

"I understand that."

"I wish I had him in court, but I'll have to make do with what I have."

"What about Tyler?"

"What about him?"

"Well, according to Ray he and Pesce were in business together."

"That's not against the law."

"That depends on what business they were in."

"I won't be bringing that up in court."

He was taking the news very calmly.

"You knew all of this, didn't you?"

"All of what?"

"Pesce told you everything. He told you it was Ray who killed Bonetti."

"Miles—"

"You wouldn't have taken the case unless he told you everything."

"Miles, I can't say any more—"

"You don't have to."

I wasn't sure how I felt at the moment. I would like to

have known that from the start, but would I have believed Pesce? I didn't know.

"Bill me for your time, Miles."

"I will."

"At our rate, not Walker's."

"We're not partners yet. Not until I sign the partnership papers."

"Oh, yes, the papers." He picked up the brown envelope the papers had been in and held it out to me. "They look fine to me. I think this is a good deal for you, Miles."

"Yeah, so do I." I took the papers. "Thanks."

"There were a couple of tapes in the envelope," he added as I headed for the door. "Missy has them."

"Fine."

"I know you're angry—"

"Then you know more than me," I said, "because I don't know what I am."

I left his office and stopped at Missy's desk.

"Is anything wrong?" She was studying my face.

"No, nothing."

"I put everything in this envelope." She handed me another brown envelope, fat and heavy with papers.

"Is this everything that was on the disk?"

"Except for that password file."

"Okay."

"Your tapes are in there also, and the disk. In fact, there are two disks. I made you another copy."

"That was smart," I said. "Thanks. As a matter of fact . . ."

I fished the other disk out of the envelope and handed it to her.

"Will you hang on to that for me?"

"Sure."

"Just put it in with the rest of yours. No one will know the difference."

She pulled over a plastic file case that was filled with disks and slid that one in among the rest.

"Great. Thanks."

"Is everything all right, Miles? I mean, between you and Heck?"

"You'll have to talk to Heck. I don't know if he's happy with my work on this case."

"Did you find Ray Carbone?"

"Talk to Heck, Missy. He's real careful about what he lets slip these days."

She wanted to talk more, but I didn't.

I was out of there.

▽

55

Vegas seemed the logical next step. I wasn't getting anything from anyone in New York, and I was depressed about what had happened with Ray. I was wishing he'd stayed to fight it out, and probably just a little disappointed in him for not doing so.

I'd call the airline later to get a ticket for Vegas. On such short notice the cost would be an arm and a leg, and I was paying for it out of my own pocket, but what the hell. I'd gone this far, and now I'd be able to devote all my attention to the one case.

I went to Packy's to tell Geneva what my plans were. I also told her about Ray's visit that morning.

"You feelin' bad?"

"Oh, yeah."

"He's doin' what he thinks is best for him, ain't he?" she asked. "That's disappoints you?"

I rubbed my hand over my face and said, "I guess."

"You'd fight, huh?"

"I'd like to think so. Life on the run doesn't appeal to me."

"So what's gonna happen in Vegas?" she asked, changing the subject.

"I don't know. I'm not finding out much here, unless there's something in here that changes my mind."

"What's that?"

"Stuff that was on Waldrop's computer. I'm going into the office to read it, and to call the airline."

"Get a charter."

"What?"

"Get a charter," she said again. "Call a travel agent and get a charter. It'll be cheaper. You'll have to fly to and from on their days, but you'll save money. This is comin' out of your own pocket, isn't it?"

"Well . . . yeah."

"Give it a try. You might be able to get a Sunday flight."

"How do you know so much?"

"Hey, I been to Vegas."

"I didn't know you were a gambler."

"I'm not. There was a bodybuilding competition there last year. I saved a lot of money flying on a charter."

"Do you remember which travel agent you used?"

"As a matter of fact, I do, 'cause I used them again after that. I'll get the number for you."

"Okay, then I'll give it a try. Thanks, Gen."

I went into the office and sat at my desk. I undid the clasp on the envelope Missy had given me and pulled out a sheaf of papers. They had come off a printer and were still joined. I didn't see any reason to separate them.

At first glance there wasn't much there. Some letters to people I'd never heard of, the contents of which did not seem germane to the incidents at hand. He also used a file for his phone book, and there were a lot of numbers there. Among them I found the number for the Healy Agency, and also Andrea Legend's home phone number. Sammy Friedlander was also there, along with Lenny James and, surprisingly, William Allegretto. I had not gotten the impression that night that Waldrop and Allegretto were friends. I tried to remember if I had asked either Allegretto or Andrea about it, but couldn't.

He had addresses in there for Billy Crystal, and Whoopi Goldberg and Robin Williams and Paul Reiser, but they were all "care of" addresses, usually listing the name and address of an agency beneath it. It was the kind of thing you'd do if you wanted to feel like you knew those people. It was more than a little sad.

I found myself wondering how good a comic Stan Waldrop had really been. His uncle didn't think much of his jokes, but he must have worked fairly often, or else why would Jonathan Healy keep him on as a client? Or did the comic keep the agent? Relationships between agents and clients always confused me. I mean, was it like a lawyer and client, where the client could fire the lawyer, but the lawyer could also refuse to work for the client? Would Waldrop fire Healy, or the other way around?

There were a couple of short stories among the papers, which surprised me. Nobody had said anything about Waldrop being a writer. I read a little bit of each and hoped he was a better comic than he was a writer.

I was sitting back in my chair, rubbing my temples, when Geneva came in.

"Headache?"

"The start of one."

"Too much reading."

"I think so."

"There's not much to read here," she said, handing me a small piece of paper. On it she'd written *Travel Well*, and a phone number.

"Thanks. I'll call them."

"Are you gonna go and see Marty this morning?"

I tried not to let show that it had completely slipped my mind.

"Yeah, this afternoon."

"I saw him before I went to work out," she said. "He's feeling better. They might let him out tomorrow."

"That's great."

"I'll bet he could use some help paying the hospital bill."

"Come on, Gen. Of course I'm going to pay his bill."

"I never doubted you, Boss," she said, and left the office.

Yeah, right.

Twenty minutes later I was booked on a charter flight from New York to Vegas, via St. Louis, for Sunday. The only problem with it was that I'd have to fly back on Thursday, or get stuck there until the following Sunday. I didn't feel that my business there would take four days, but booking a commercial flight would have cost almost twice as much, and I did have a dead client, didn't I? Couldn't very well submit a bill for expenses, could I?

With that done, I put away the papers from Stan Waldrop's computer. I'd have plenty of time on the flight, and in Vegas, to go over them. Instead, I took out the partnership papers from Walker and read them over. Then, with Heck Delgado's assurance that they were in order, and since I hadn't found anything I objected to, I signed them. Now all I had to do was get them to Walker so that the partnership was signed, sealed, and delivered. I thought about sending a messenger over to his office—his old office—with them, but then decided to do it myself.

I didn't have much else to do before my flight, and that was two days away.

▽

56

I WENT OVER to Walker's office without calling first, but I was in luck and found him in. There were boxes all over the place, filled with files, as he got himself ready for the move. I wondered if I was supposed to bring any files with me. I hoped that wasn't a deal breaker, because I didn't have many.

I was standing in the outer office when he came walking out.

"Hello, Miles. As you can see, we're getting ready."

"I can see."

He looked at the envelope in my hand and asked, "Are those the papers?"

"Yes, they are." I handed them to him.

"I hadn't heard from you. I thought perhaps you were changing your mind."

"No, actually I've been pretty busy."

"You took on some cases?"

"More like they took me on."

"Anything I can help with?"

I hesitated.

"I hadn't called you because they were sort of odd cases, and since we hadn't signed any papers—"

"Why don't you come inside and tell me about them?"

"Okay," I said, "okay, maybe talking about them would help. Maybe you can come up with something I haven't, so far. Actually, one of them has sort of solved itself . . ."

* * *

"And you consider this case with Ray Carbone solved?" Walker asked when I finished talking.

"Ray's leaving town, Walker. Would you call that solved?"

"Well, I know Ray Carbone, but not as well as you do."

I waited a few seconds and then said, "But?"

Walker shrugged. "He never struck me as the kind of man to run."

"Not even if it was the smart thing to do?"

"Men rarely do the smart thing, Miles. I'm sure you've noticed that."

"Noticed it? I'm a prime example."

"Then what makes you think Ray Carbone is going to do the smart thing?"

I stared at him for a long time.

"He was scamming me."

Walker shrugged. "Maybe. Think about it. Now this other case intrigues me. I wish you had called me sooner."

I started to explain again why I hadn't, but he waved the explanation away.

"We started out thinking some jokes had been stolen from a computer, but it's obvious now that we're dealing with something much more serious."

We? Maybe this partnership stuff was an even better idea than I'd first thought.

"Let me ask you something," he said.

"What?"

"Do you think Stan Waldrop thought there was something more at stake than his jokes when he first came to you?"

I frowned. "He seemed sincere, but considering I was scammed by a friend in Ray—"

"Put that aside for now. Think back to your initial interview with Waldrop."

I sat back and closed my eyes, envisioning Stan Waldrop sitting across from me.

"There was real panic in his eyes, Walker. He thought his

career was going to be over because someone had stolen his act."

"So even if there is something more serious afoot, and even if he was part of it, he was there that day simply because of his, uh, jokes."

I opened my eyes.

"I believe so."

"So by hiring you he apparently frightened someone enough to make them kill him. Somebody thought that by poking around looking for his jokes, you were going to turn up something else."

"Then why not kill me?"

"Too risky, perhaps. They thought it better to kill him before you could even get started on your investigation. They had no idea you'd be tenacious enough to continue, even after your client was dead."

"Okay, all of that could be true, but what was he really into? What was it that got him killed?"

"Perhaps your trip to Las Vegas will turn up something. Do you have the disk and the message tapes with you?"

"Yes." I had stuck them in my pocket out of force of habit before leaving Packy's.

"Why don't you leave them with me while you go to Vegas? My computer equipment is still set up. Maybe I can break into that password file."

It was a good idea, so I took them out and gave them to him. He set them aside on his desk.

"By the time you return, we will be in our new suite up on the fifteenth floor."

"Fifteen," I said, wondering if I'd get nosebleeds working at that height.

"Is that a problem?"

"No, no," I said, "I've just never had that kind of view of the city before."

"What about your bar?"

"My bar? What about it?"

"You do intend to keep it, don't you?"

"Well . . . I hadn't decided yet."

"Why wouldn't you?"

"Well, I didn't know how you'd feel about being partners with a bar owner."

"That's nonsense. If you like running it and want to keep it, then you should. You probably have an office in the back."

"I do, but it's nothing like this, nothing like what we'll have on the fifteenth floor."

"Miles, just because we're partners doesn't mean I expect you to come in here every day."

"You don't?"

"No. You are not my employee. You come in when you want—as long as we're making money, that is."

"Of course."

"As long as we both bring in cases, and we are profitable, this partnership will work. I think you should keep the bar—Packy's, isn't it—as long as you like. You might even be more comfortable working out of there for a while. You could . . . ease into your office on the fifteenth floor."

"That might not be a bad idea."

"I wish I could help you more with these cases, Miles. Perhaps I'll know more when you get back from Vegas."

"You've already helped a lot, Walker." I stood up. "Thanks very much."

He stood up and we shook hands.

"Have a good trip . . . partner."

$\triangledown$

57

OH YEAH, WALKER had helped me a lot. He helped me realize what a boob Ray Carbone had made of me. Of course he wasn't leaving town, he was just trying to throw me off—and he'd succeeded, up until now.

And I'd given that sonofabitch my emergency stein money.

I found a pay phone and called Heck Delgado's office. It was my lucky day. His court appearance had been cancelled and he was in.

"Miles, I'm sorry if you left angry this morning—"

"Forget it. You can make it up to me with a favor."

"What kind of favor?"

I explained about thinking that Ray Carbone had been conning me, but I didn't tell him that it had come from Walker. I wasn't trying to protect myself from looking stupid—okay, maybe I was—I was just keeping the explanations down to a minimum.

"What do you want me to do?"

"I don't want you to tell anyone about my meeting with Ray."

He hesitated only a second and then said, "Done. Are you going to continue to look for Ray?"

"Yes."

"I'll need him by next week, Jack."

Shit. I didn't want to tell him that I'd be in Vegas all next week.

"I might have something for you tomorrow, Heck. Why

don't you give me your number at home so I can call you if something breaks?"

"All right." He gave me the number and I wrote it in my notebook.

"I'll call you as soon as I know something."

We hung up, and I stood there a moment wondering why I had, in effect, just given myself the rest of today and all of tomorrow to find Ray when the only time I'd seen him all week was when he found me.

I had to find Ray before I left for Vegas, there was no two ways about it.

Just for a minute I thought about going home, or going to Packy's to call Nick Delvecchio about Truman Tyler, and then decided just to do it right from the pay phone.

"Jack," he said, picking up on the first ring, "you just caught me. I was on my way out."

Shit. I wanted to talk to him now.

"Do you want to call me later?"

"No, I can talk. Is this about Tyler?"

"Yeah, Nick. I hope you found something out."

"I did, something that might even help you."

"Like what?"

"Like Tyler is married to the mob."

"How so?"

"Well, his wife is the daughter of a second cousin—oh hell, it's confusing, especially if you're not Italian. What it all boils down to is that Truman Tyler's wife's maiden name is Bonetti."

"What?" A truck had gone by at that moment and I wasn't sure I'd heard him correctly.

"I said, Truman Tyler's wife, Angela, is—or was—Michael Bonetti's sister."

"And Tyler is trying to help get Danny Pesce off for killing him?"

Nick hesitated a moment and then said, "Is he?"

$\triangledown$

58

I COULD HAVE waited for Saturday to go looking for Truman Tyler, but something told me to hop the subway to Brooklyn now and try to catch him in his office. If I waited for tomorrow I'd have to try to catch him at home, and even though Delvecchio managed to get the address for me, I didn't look forward to that. I wanted to deal with Tyler, not his wife and her family.

From Delvecchio I learned that the Bonettis were not high ranking in the Mafia, but they were "Family," and that was what mattered. For killing Michael Bonetti, Danny Pesce would have to pay—he was there—as would Ray Carbone who, according to Pesce, did the actual killing.

I had to believe that Ray killed Bonetti. Why would he lie about it? It had probably happened just the way he'd said it had, though, accidentally, but the boys wouldn't accept that.

Unless . . .

Unless I could prove that Bonetti was stealing from them. For that, I needed Truman Tyler's cooperation.

Willing or unwilling.

When I got to Court Street, it was starting to empty out. There were many more people going down into the subway stations than there were coming up. Not only were the legal and medical offices belching forth people, but the court-houses as well. It was like trying to walk against a strong tide in some places, but I finally made it to Tyler's office.

I mounted the steps to his office and tried the door. It was locked, but the lights were on inside. Standing on my toes I could see that his outer office was as empty and dusty as it had been the last time I was there, but there seemed to be shadows moving in his office. I knocked and the shadows stopped moving. I knocked again and there was no answer. I now figured that Tyler and whoever was in there with him were pretending they weren't there in the hopes that whoever was knocking—me—would go away.

Fat chance.

I pounded on the door, and Tyler finally appeared, looking nervous, and opened it a crack.

"Jacoby?"

"You want to pretend you're not here, Tyler, you better get yourself a real office door, without a window. Then again, a real door would look out of place here, wouldn't it?"

"Go away."

"Let me in."

"I—I can't."

"Why not?"

"I—office hours are over."

"You're the boss," I said. "You can give yourself overtime. Come on, we've got to talk."

"About what?"

"Ray Carbone, Danny Pesce, and your brother-in-law, Michael Bonetti."

"It's no secret that Mike was my brother-in-law."

"I'll bet Ray Carbone didn't know it, did he? When you and Pesce roped him into whatever your scheme was."

"No scheme," Tyler said. "Ray was hired to protect Danny, that was all."

"Like Danny Pesce really needed protection from somebody? Come on, Tyler, Ray was your fall guy, but you didn't expect Bonetti to get killed, did you?"

"Go away, damn it—"

"Let him in," a voice said from inside. I recognized it.

Tyler sighed, stepped back, and I went inside. Standing in the doorway to Tyler's office was a man with a gun.

"Hello, Jack."

"Didn't get very far," I said, "did you, Ray?"

▽

59

"COULD YOU POINT that somewhere else, Ray? Unless it's meant for me too?"

"Don't be an asshole." He lowered the gun, but did not put it away.

"He's crazy," Tyler said hurriedly. "He's going to kill me."

"Is that right, Ray? Are you going to kill him?"

"He's going to tell me who killed Joy," Ray said. "I mean, who actually tortured her and beat her and killed her."

"I don't know anything about that," Tyler said. "I swear."

"Oh, shut up, Truman," I said. "Sure you do. It was you and Danny who set this up and brought Ray into it. That right, Ray?"

"That's right. Danny hired me because he said he was afraid of Mike Bonetti."

"What happened that night, Ray?"

"I told you the truth about that, Jack. They came at us and I did what I do, you know? Bonetti died because of it. It was more their fault than mine."

"What's the counselor here have to say about it all?"

"He says he doesn't know anything about it."

"Well, that's that, then. Let's go."

"What?" Ray was staring at me as if I was crazy.

Tyler looked relieved.

"Yeah, that's right, get him out of here." He was getting brave. "He's lucky I don't call the police."

"Jack, are you—"

"Hey, Ray, if he says he doesn't know anything about it, then he doesn't."

"Jack—"

"But I think he'll have a harder time convincing Mike Bonetti's family of that."

Ray stared at me, then smiled.

"What?" Tyler asked.

"Bonetti's family—I mean, your wife's family. How are they going to feel when they find out you had something to do with his death?"

"What are you talking about? Who—who's gonna tell 'em?"

His Brooklyn accent, the one he tried desperately to hide when he was in lawyer mode, was starting to come out.

"We are. Look, Truman, we know you were involved and your brother-in-law ended up dead. Maybe we can't prove it, but you know how your wife's family is. They won't need proof. Come on, Ray."

Ray started to follow me to the door.

"Wait a minute, wait a minute." Tyler was waving his arms in front of him as if trying to dispel the words he had just heard. "Wait, wait . . ."

"For what, Truman?" I asked.

"Lemme think, lemme think . . ."

"There's no time to think, Truman. You and Danny went into business for yourselves, and you were trying to bring Mike in. Mike didn't go for it, and he warned you not to get involved. Since he was the only one in the 'Family' who knew, you had to get rid of him, or eventually you knew he'd spill the beans, brother-in-law or no."

"No, no," Tyler said, "I never meant for Mike to get killed. Jesus, no, Angela would never forgive me."

"Being forgiven by your wife would seem to be the least of your problems, Tyler. You told your family that Ray and Danny killed Mike, didn't you?"

"No," he said, looking away, "not Danny."

"You guys were going to take up where you left off when he got out?"

"You sonofabitch!" Ray said with feeling. "He was going to give me up, wasn't he? After he played the stand-up guy for a while?"

"Yeah," Tyler said, still not looking at us. "Yeah, he was, but by then . . ."

"By then they figured you'd already be dead, Ray," I finished. "Bonetti's family would have gotten to you by then."

"Or you'd be gone," Tyler said, "and they'd spend a long time looking for you."

"Meanwhile, you and Danny continue your business, whatever it was."

"It was—"

"I don't *care* what it was!" Ray shouted. He brought his cannon out again and pointed it at Tyler. "I just want the cocksucker who killed Joy!"

Tyler's eyes widened as he stared at the gun. He was frightened out of his wits now. Frightened of Bonetti's family, of his own wife, and of Ray and his gun.

"Wait, wait, wait!" he said, holding his hands out. "Wait."

"Wait for what?"

"I can't think, damn it!"

"That's your problem, isn't it?" I asked.

"No, that's not his problem." Ray closed the ground between himself and Tyler and pressed the barrel of his gun underneath the lawyer's chin. "This is his problem."

Right at that moment there was a knock on the door. No, not a knock, more like a pounding.

"Who's that?" I asked Tyler.

"That's the man you're looking for," Tyler said, looking at Ray. "The man who killed your girl."

"What's he doing here?" I asked. "Jesus, Ray, did you call Tyler before you came?"

"It was the only way to get him to meet me."

I looked at Tyler. "And you called your men?"

"Not my men. My family."

"Truman, open the damn door!" a man called.

"How many?" I asked Tyler.

He didn't answer.

"How many?" Ray repeated, pressing the barrel of the gun so hard against Tyler's flesh that I knew he'd be wearing a circle in his skin for a while.

"Four," he said, "there'll be four."

"What's the man's name?" Ray asked. "The one who killed Joy?"

"I don't know."

"Tyler—"

"I don't," Tyler insisted. "I only know it was one of the four of them. They've been looking for you since—"

"Since you gave him up," I said. "Is there another way out of here?"

"Not unless you want to go out a window."

"You carrying?" Ray asked.

"Yeah."

I'd clipped my .38 to my belt that morning before I left home. I didn't relish having to use it, but I wouldn't have worn it if I wasn't willing to.

"Truman, you in there?"

"What's his name?" Ray asked.

"Olivetti."

"Olivetti!" Ray called out.

There was a moment of silence and then the man answered. "Yeah?"

"This is Ray Carbone. I'm coming out."

"Come ahead."

"I want you and your men down the stairs, or I'll put a bullet in Tyler's head."

"They don't care about me," Tyler said, resigned.

"We're gonna find out if you're right," Ray said.

"We going out?" I asked.

"We're goin' out."

I took my gun out of the holster. It felt alien in my hand. I was used to holding it on the shooting range, not in situations like this.

"Oh, one thing," Ray said.

"What?"

"Here."

He took his left hand out of his jacket pocket and handed me some money.

"That's the money you gave me," he said. "Just in case we don't make it I don't want that on my conscience."

I stared down at my stein money and then shoved it into my pocket.

"I'm glad you feel better."

"Shall we go?"

▽

60

I GOT THE door, but Ray went out first, with Tyler in front of him. I don't think either of us really thought they'd shoot Tyler, so I'll bet Ray was as surprised as I was when they started shooting immediately. I heard a sound similar to one I used to hear in the ring. Then it was leather striking flesh and tearing open a cut. This time it was lead slamming into meat.

Tyler cried out and slumped in Ray's grasp, but Ray held him up with one hand. I came out the door and looked down the steps. There were four men at the bottom, and they weren't finished shooting.

Ray began firing, and I pointed my gun and started pulling the trigger, probably with less results. Ray's gun was larger, made more noise, and was probably being fired more accurately. I still didn't hold out much hope for us surviving this, until suddenly the four men looked around. One of them spun and staggered, one of the others catching him before he could fall. I realized then that someone besides us was firing at them, and they realized it too.

There was a big man among them and he shouted at them something that could have been, "Let's get out of here," or "Go fuck yourself in your ear." Whatever he said, they all turned and took off, leaving us standing at the top of the stairs with a bleeding Truman Tyler.

"Stand up, Tyler," Ray said, roughly. "You're not hit that bad."

Ray released Tyler, who slumped against the side of the building clutching his bleeding right arm.

"You hit?" Ray asked me.

"No."

"Good, that makes one of us," he said, and then he fell.

▽

61

On a plane to Las Vegas Sunday I was thinking back to the events of Friday night. It was difficult to do, because on a charter people are gregarious and want to talk. Also, it seems many of them know each other. However, once I convinced my seatmate that I didn't want to talk—a dirty look did it—I was able to close my eyes and concentrate....

As it turned out, the slug I heard hit ended up in Ray's right shoulder. His wound was worse than Tyler's, but I got both of them inside and seated and called for an ambulance. Shots fired on a Brooklyn street—especially one like Court Street—bring the police fairly quickly, but when I called 911 for the ambulance I also asked for the cops.

While I was doing that, Nick Delvecchio came into the office. He was the one who had been shooting at the four men downstairs. He waited until I got off the phone to speak, taking the opportunity to try to help Ray with his wound.

"They left one behind. He's dead."

"Me or you?" I asked, holding my breath.

"I got him, Jack. You all right?"

"Thanks to you. What are you doing here?"

He shrugged and said, "I had a feeling you'd be coming here without backup."

"What made you think I'd need backup?"

He shrugged again and said, "Instinct."

"Good instincts. Thanks, Nick."

"Any time."

He waited with us for the police, who arrived before the ambulance. They started taking statements, and when the first ambulance crew arrived I made sure they took Ray before Tyler. When the second crew removed Tyler, the cops went to the hospital to continue taking statements. A morgue wagon came and took the dead man. Later he'd be identified as a "low-ranking" member of the Mafia.

Delvecchio and I gave statements at the scene to two detectives Nick knew. Their names were Weinstock and Matucci. He seemed friendly enough with the first, but at odds with the second.

We all went down to the precinct then, and sat around talking for most of the night. They also took the opportunity to check both Nick's and my carry permit for our guns.

When they finally let us go, Weinstock assured me that he'd be checking with the Manhattan cops on the Danny Pesce and Joy White cases.

By the time I boarded the plane this is what I knew: Ray was now in custody for his part in the Bonetti murder. He'd never intended to run. Before he gave himself up, he only wanted to find the man who killed Joy. Now that he had a name—Olivetti—he was willing to go to court to clear himself, knowing that he could find the man when it was all over. Heck Delgado agreed—in the Saturday phone call to his house placed by me—to represent Ray.

Truman Tyler was still professing his innocence in both of the murders, but he was admitting to being partners with Danny Pesce rather than simply his lawyer. He also didn't want to be released from the hospital without police protection.

I left New York feeling certain that Heck would do his best for Ray, and that things would be sorted out, maybe even by the time I got back. I had done my part, I had found Ray, and now I was going to concentrate on fulfilling whatever obligation I had left to Stanley Waldrop.

I managed to get off the plane without having to have a conversation with any of the degenerate gamblers getting off the plane with glazed eyes, heading directly for the slot machines in the terminal. Since I had taken a small carry-on bag, I was able to head right for a cabstand and get a taxi to the Aladdin. The marquee outside the hotel announced the appearance of George Thoroughgood and Depeche Mode during that week. I felt certain they would not be there on the same night, and that they would not draw the same crowd.

The Aladdin is one of the midsize casino hotels in Vegas, certainly not in a class with the new MGM Grand—which was just down the street—or the Luxor, or the old standbys like the Golden Nugget, the Stardust, the Riviera, or Bugsy's place, the Flamingo. Still, I couldn't fathom what a stand-up comic of Stan Waldrop's stature had been doing performing here. A David Brenner or George Carlin maybe, but Stan Waldrop? Somebody must have pulled some strings to get him here, and probably for a reason other than his comedic talent.

The Aladdin had a high-rise section and a three-story annex. I managed to get a room in the annex for $29.00 a night on special, thanks to the travel agency that had booked the charter. Geneva had saved me a bundle with that suggestion. The hotel probably felt they could offer a room rate that low because their guests would be dropping a bundle in the casino.

They hadn't figured on me, though. I didn't gamble much, and being in Vegas wasn't going to change that a whole lot. I enjoy an occasional poker night with friends, and a bet on a horse during a big race like the Kentucky Derby. I've even been to the track with the friends once or twice—Henry Po once, and Nick Delvecchio once—and I'd gone with Po because he worked for the racing association and got me in for free.

I deposited my bag in my room and went back down to the casino. My strategy was simple. I would use Eddie's book to find myself a PI in Las Vegas who knew somebody in security at the Aladdin. The closest I got was a woman named Freddie O'Neal who lived and worked in Reno. As it happened, she knew somebody who knew somebody, and I took the elevator down to the main floor and started looking for him. I asked at the desk where security was, and after I convinced them that I was not having a problem with the casino or the hotel itself, they directed me.

His name was Kyle Morgan, and when I saw that he wore a suit and not a uniform, I assumed he wasn't just a security guard.

"What can I do for you, Mr. Jacoby?" he asked while we shook hands.

"Don't you want to see my ID?"

"You were described to me, sir. Just tell me how I can help you."

"I will, but don't call me 'sir', okay, Kyle?"

"Okay, Miles."

I told him that Stan Waldrop had been killed in New York, and that this was the last place he worked.

"I remember him."

That surprised me.

"Why?"

"I caught his act one night. I'm no critic, but I know what I like. He was bad."

"How bad?"

"So bad that I figured there had to be another reason he was here. I thought it might be gambling, but if he gambled he didn't do it here."

"Did you see him with anyone?"

"Oh, sure. His friend was the one who gambled."

"His friend? Could you describe him?"

"Sure, easy. He was an older man with bad teeth and a bad toupee. I heard some of the dealers say that he never shut up, just keep telling jokes the whole time he was gambling."

"Did people complain?"

"Hell, no. They were too busy laughing. Apparently this guy was a lot better than Waldrop."

"I see."

It was pretty clear who the friend was. I doubted that Sam Friedlander had flown to Vegas just to catch his nephew's act, so now it seemed that Stan and his uncle Sammy had both been there for some reason that had nothing to do with comedy.

A reason that had gotten Stan killed.

"Thanks very much, Kyle."

Morgan looked surprised.

"That's it? That's all you wanted?"

"No, but as it turns out," I said, "it might be all I need."

∇

62

"How can you say a charter was a bad idea?" Geneva complained.

"I found out what I needed to know within the first two hours I was there, but I still had to stay until Thursday."

"So? You still saved money on the flight and the hotel."

"I probably lost more than I saved on those stupid slot machines."

"Well," she said, with her arms folded across her chest, "who told you to gamble?"

"What else was there to do?"

"See some shows."

"They cost money too."

In fact, I had caught a show—two, but that was enough. I had even walked around and watched the volcano erupt in front of the Mirage, and the pirate boat battle in front of Treasure Island. I had seen the MGM Grand, and the Luxor, and the Excaliber, and while I was seeing them I was dropping quarters—okay, and then dollars—into the slot machines.

I had even gone to a girlie place called Glitter Gulch, but after a couple of hours of putting dollar bills between breasts, even that got boring.

This was Friday and I had gotten back late the night before. All I'd done so far was call Heck and tell him I was back. Actually, he wasn't in, so I left the message with Missy. She couldn't—or wouldn't—tell me anything about the

Danny Pesce case, or what was happening with Ray Carbone. I'd have to hear that from Heck himself.

I had hauled out Eddie's trusty book after breakfast and
made some calls. I hoped to have some callbacks later that
day so that I could catch Sammy Freed at one of his deli
stops. That was why I was stuck to the phone at Packy's,
arguing with Geneva about what I should or should not have
done in Vegas.

"Well, what about some of those legal pussy parlors? You
mean you didn't try one of them out?"

The legal chicken farms in Vegas were plentiful, and they
advertised in flyers that were free on every street corner.

"There were so many, I didn't know which one to choose."

"Hey, some of them even come to your room. What about
that?"

"I'm not in the habit of paying for sex, Gen."

"Hey, Vegas is Vegas. You got to enjoy it to the fullest."

"Wait a minute," I said. "They even have guys who come
to your room. I saw that in some of the flyers. You mean that
you—"

She held up a hand to stop me. "A girl's got to try
everything . . . at least once."

"You didn't!" I said, but she just smiled and went to
unlock the door to let the day's business begin.

The first person through the door was Steve Stilwell, and
he was obviously happy.

"From the looks of you, things have gone your way," I said.

"IAD dropped its investigation," he said. "Bruce and I
were reinstated this morning."

"Well, good for you. Where is the big lug? I'll buy you both
a drink."

"He's celebrating with the lovely Veronica."

"The lovely Veronica" was Taylor's new love. According
to him, she was his last love too. He'd gotten divorced some
years back, badly, and Veronica was the first woman to make
him forget how painful it had really been.

"Good for him. I'll buy you a drink, then."

"Why not? I don't have anyone to celebrate with—unless—" He was looking Geneva's way.

"Don't even think it," she said, putting a Rolling Rock in front of him. "I got better things to do with my time than entertain your skinny white ass."

"So it's just you and me," Steve said to me. "When did you get back?"

"Last night."

"Did the trip help?"

"I think so, but I won't be sure for a while. I'm waiting for some information."

"What kind of information?"

"Airline. I need to know if someone flew to Vegas last week."

"Why didn't you ask? I know somebody in airport security. He can get into any of the airline's computers. What's the name you're looking for?"

"More than one," I said, and gave them all to him.

"Geneva, the phone, please," he said imperiously.

"Walk around here and use it," she said. "I ain't your slave, honey."

With a less than imperious look he walked around the bar, used the phone, and got me the information I needed within the hour.

I thanked him, gave him carte blanche in my absence, and went to see what deli Sammy Freed was at today.

▽

63

I'M A DETECTIVE, that's how I figured Sammy Freed was either at the New York Deli, or the Carnegie Deli. I'd already seen him twice, at the Stage and at Wolf's, so I figured today he'd be at one of the others. I tried the New York, and he was there, at one of the tables on a balcony. Sometimes this business of deduction really works.

"It's the honest Shamus," he said when I appeared at his table. "Where you been all week? It ain't been the same without you."

I sat down. "I was in Vegas."

Freed stared at me for a moment before speaking,

"Did you win? How much did they take you for?"

"A bundle, but it was worth it. I stayed at the Aladdin, Sammy, where Stan played last."

"Stan at the Aladdin, huh? He must have a good agent."

"They remember you there, Sammy. You're hard not to remember, you know."

"Sure, I know," he said, grimacing and waving a hand at me. "I gotta get a hairpiece that fits. You think I don't know it don't fit? That it looks like a fucking throw rug?"

"I'm thinking you killed Stan, Sammy." It came from out of the blue, for him and for me. "Why am I thinking you killed your nephew?"

"The putz."

"Your nephew the putz."

He stared at me for a few moments, ignoring the remains of his brisket sandwich.

"I wish I had a gun, you know?"

"Why? What would you do? Shoot me?"

"Naw, naw," he said, waving both hands. "It's me I'd shoot, not you."

"Did you kill him, Sammy?"

"Sure, I killed him. Who else would kill him?"

His admission surprised me.

"You said he had a lot of enemies."

"Not people who would kill him."

"Why did you kill him?"

"It was an accident. We argued, he got me all worked up, and I hit him." He shrugged. "An accident. My sister's boy." He shook his head.

"What was the argument about?"

"Same thing we been arguing about for months. He was writing a book."

"What kind of book?"

" 'The King of The Catskills', he called it. It was about me."

"A biography?"

"Sure, whatever you call it."

"Why the argument?"

"I didn't want him to write it, but he was doing it anyway."

"It was an unauthorized biography?"

"I didn't want him to write it. Wouldn't you call that unauthorized?"

"Why didn't you want him to write it?"

"Because he was gonna talk about things I'd rather forget, that's why."

"I'm a little confused, Sammy. Was this some kind of tell-all book?"

"Sure, he was gonna tell everything."

"What would have been so bad? I mean—I'm sorry, but did you have that interesting a career? Or life?"

He waited a moment, then said, "Look, Mr. Detective,

back when I was trying to make it in this business you had to do things you didn't want to do, you know? To get on that circuit you had to play by the rules."

"And who made the rules, Sammy?"

"Who else? The people who are still making them."

"The Mafia?"

"The Mafia. Back then they were called the 'Mob', the 'Syndicate'. What do they call them now? Wise Guys? Always they're coming up with new names, these Italians."

"What else? What else was in the book?"

"I don't know what was in the goddamn book. That's what I was trying to find out, but he wouldn't tell me. He said I'd read about it when everybody else did."

"Did he have a publisher for it yet?"

"I don't think so. If he did, he woulda told me, just to rub it in."

I was still confused. Could it be that Sammy Freed had been bigger than I remembered? Come to think of it, I didn't remember him all that well.

"I know what you're thinkin'," Freed said, staring at me. "So you don't remember me, so what? I was big back then, Mr. Detective, and getting bigger."

"What happened?"

"I stepped in shit, that's what happened. I got caught shtupping the wrong twist."

"And that did it? That did in your career?"

"Ha!" he said. "It almost got me killed too."

I didn't know whether to believe him or not.

"Sammy, you and your nephew, you didn't get along?"

"Get along with a putz? How do you get along with such a man?"

"So you killed him."

"I told you, it was an accident."

Accusing him of the murder was a shot in the dark, but now that he was admitting it I didn't buy the accidental part of it. Not knowing what I knew.

"Sammy, why'd you go to Vegas?"

"Why? To talk to him, that's why. How do you think he got booked into Vegas?"

"You?"

"Sure, me. Who else? I know people, I got him booked. I wanted to show him I could help him."

"Did you ever help him before?"

"No," Freed said, "nobody helped me when I was trying to break in. I had to take all my lumps, dealing with those cocksuckers—you should excuse the expression."

"So Stan was angry that you didn't help him?"

"Always, he was mad, but I thought it would make a man of him, you know? Instead he became a nasty little shit!"

"Sammy," I said slowly, "if you'll excuse me for saying so, I don't think you killed him by accident."

"You're the hotshot detective. Why do you say that?"

"Because I happen to know you flew to L.A. and then rented a car and drove to Vegas."

I knew he had flown to L.A. thanks to Steve Stilwell. The part about the rented car was another shot in the dark.

"You didn't want any record that you were in Vegas. That sounds to me like you meant to kill him, maybe even there."

He didn't respond.

"How am I doing?"

"Do you know who got John Healy to keep Stanley on when he was gonna dump him? Me. Uncle Sammy. Who got him the job in the Village? Me. Who got him Vegas? Me."

"Apparently, Stan thought this was all too little, too late, Sammy."

He pointed a finger at me and said, "That's what the little shit said to me. Then he turned around and I hit him."

"With what?"

"Huh?"

"What did you hit him with?"

"I don't know. I picked something up, something that was there."

"And then what?"

"I dropped it and ran."

"And nobody saw you?"

"Who was looking? They're all so busy putting on their show. like you could call what these comics do today a show. Filth, that's what they call humor, these days. They all think they're Lenny Bruce. Lemme tell you, there was only one Lenny Bruce."

"Sammy, how did you get out of the club without being seen?"

"I got in and out because of this," he said, pointing to the rug on this head. "I took it off, and wore glasses, and walked in and out like a doddering old fool. Nobody recognized me."

Not even me. I didn't remember seeing anyone remotely resembling Sammy that night, but he'd been there and I'd missed him.

"Sammy, you're still lying. There was no murder weapon found at the scene."

"So maybe I took it with me."

"And dropped it along the way?"

"I guess."

"Nothing was found in the neighborhood. I think you had your weapon with you, and when he turned around you used it. What was it? A gun? You knew a shot would be heard so you hit him with it? Or a blackjack? What?"

Sammy Freed's look became crafty.

"If it was a gun, maybe I'd still have it on me."

We stared at each other for a few moments.

"I'll ask you what I asked you earlier. Are you going to shoot me with it?"

"I don't have a gun."

"I do."

"What? Now you're trying to scare me?"

"You intended to kill me, didn't you, Sammy?"

"I don't say nothin' no more without my lawyer."

"You want to call him now, or when we get to the police station?"

"What, call him now," he said, "the *gonif*, he'd put me on the clock from the minute he picked up the phone. From the police station I'll call him, and I ain't goin' on the clock until he gets there. Lawyers, they're all crooks. Did you hear the one about the three lawyers havin' lunch together? One lawyer says to the other two . . ."

▽

Epilogue

WHEN THEY TOOK Sam Friedlander, aka Sammy Freed, into custody he was carrying an old army .45 tucked into his waistband. If he had taken it out at the New York Deli, he and I would probably have made a mess in some kind of Wild West shoot-out. I probably would have ended up dead. Instead, he tried to kill me with bad jokes on the way to the nearest precinct.

Later they determined that Freed had indeed clubbed his nephew to death with the .45. It was probably also what he had used to hit Marty with at Waldrop's apartment. Sammy was there trying to find the book that his nephew was writing about him. It was questionable whether Waldrop would even have been able to sell the thing to a publisher. Sammy killed his nephew over a worthless manuscript that never would have seen the light of day anyway.

I know the manuscript was worthless because Walker Blue had cracked the password—"jokes"—to that computer file while I was in Vegas, and had printed it out, all three hundred pages of it. I thought the short stories I'd read from Waldrop's computer were bad, but this was even worse. I gave Sammy a copy so he could read it in prison.

(Walker had found something else, as well, something that had to do with Ray's case. He did something I had never done. He listened to the other side of Ray's message tape. Doing that had not dawned on me, but that's why Walker gets the big bucks. There were some messages on there from

Tyler, and from Pesce, during which they mentioned Mike
Bonetti. He had even heard the name "Olivetti" once. We
turned the tape over to the police working the Bonetti
case.)

Andrea Legend's real name turned out to be Andrea
Chaiken. She was a little Jewish girl who had grown up
calling Sammy Freed "Uncle Sammy," even though her
mother claimed that Sammy was the girl's father. Apparently
Sammy had cut himself a wide swath as a younger and not
so younger man. After all, it was what he said kept him from
becoming big, "shtupping" the wrong woman.

Andrea told me later that while Sammy had never ac-
knowledged her as his daughter, he had gotten her the job
at John Healy's agency. Healy, as it turned out, had once
represented Sammy Freed, which is how Sammy also got
Healy to hang on to Waldrop when Healy wanted to drop
him. The fact that Waldrop ended up being represented by
Healy at all was a coincidence, but one that Sammy tried to
cash in on. He had Andrea place Waldrop at the club in the
Village, and at the Aladdin, and even had her trying to
sweet-talk Stanley into showing her the manuscript. Her
planned seduction of me, which had gone awry, was on
Sammy's behalf. Sammy didn't want anyone else finding
that manuscript and was afraid that I would.

As for the missing jokes—well, that was a joke in itself.

"There were no jokes," I told Geneva.

"What?"

"Sammy thinks Waldrop made that up and hired me
because he thought it might get him some publicity."

We were in Packy's on a slow afternoon, and I had just
finished explaining the various parts of the case to her.

"What kind of publicity?"

"Any kind. Waldrop apparently thought he'd be able to use
the publicity to sell the book, but he got killed before he had
the chance."

"Too bad for Sammy that Waldrop hired you, huh?"

"Yeah, too bad."

"What's your problem, Boss?"

"I kind of liked the old guy, bad jokes and all."

"He turned out to be a killer."

"I know, but that doesn't make him a bad person."

"Is that a joke?"

"A small one."

"A very small one."

She got me an Icehouse, and herself a tonic water.

"What's happening with Ray?"

"Heck's really working hard on that one. He's trying to plea-bargain for Ray as well as make a deal with the DA for Ray's assistance in catching the men who killed Joy. Her killing was deliberate, while his killing of Bonetti was accidental."

I knew Ray would try to help the cops find Olivetti, whoever he was. If they couldn't do it, he would probably do it.

"Yeah," she said, "he was beating him up and hit him too hard. Some accident—I know, I know, he's your friend, but you gotta admit, if he wasn't beating up on the guy it never would have happened."

"I guess not, but that's Ray's work, Geneva."

"Man gets out of this one he ought to look for a new line of work."

"I guess so."

"Hey, Marty's coming to work today. First day back."

"That's great."

"You decide what you gonna do with this place now that you big time?"

I looked around and said, "I kind of like it, thought I'd keep it a while longer."

"About time you made that decision. You know, I got some more ideas about bringing in new customers."

"We'll talk about them sometime."

"No, wait, listen to this. We start havin' entertainment."

"What kind of entertainment? Girls?"

"I wouldn't work here if you hired those kinds of girls," she said, very definitely . "No, I was thinking more along the lines of live entertainment. You know, like . . . stand-up comics?"